Nina was more than halfway down the block when she suddenly decided that whether Angela wanted her there or not, she simply couldn't leave the poor woman alone to nurse her misery and rage. She turned and began to retrace her steps. It was as she started to mount the stairs to Angela's house that she heard the scream from inside.

Nina took the remaining few steps two at a time and began ringing the doorbell furiously, but Angela didn't answer. Then she pounded on the door, loudly calling Angela's name. Seemingly endless minutes passed until the door slowly opened a crack, and Angela's stricken face appeared.

"Angela, I heard a scream. What is it? What's wrong?"

Angela opened the door a little farther, and Nina nervously sidled past her. "Angela, please, what is it? Tell me!"

Angela silently pointed down a long entrance hall, past an imposing staircase that dominated the foyer. Light streamed from an open door. Nina hurried toward the room and, bracing herself, dashed through the doorway. Her first glimpse of the room brought into focus a black grand piano, a fringed white shawl draped across the closed lid. A bouquet of dark red roses was centrally and dramatically placed on top of it.

Then she saw the body.

As Nina crept closer, she realized that it was Evan Greer. Fighting fear and revulsion, she knelt to feel his pulse.

"Don't bother," Angela said tonelessly as she drifted into the room. "He's dead."

Take One for Murder

Eileen Fulton's
A SETTING
for MURDER

IVY BOOKS • NEW YORK

To Merrill Lemmon,
who made this book possible
just by being himself

Grateful acknowledgment is made
to Garin Wolf
for his editorial advice and counsel.

Ivy Books
Published by Ballantine Books

Produced by Butterfield Press, Inc.
133 Fifth Avenue
New York, New York 10003

Back cover photograph: Tom Gates

Library of Congress Catalog Card Number: 88-91129

ISBN 0-8041-0208-2

Manufactured in the United States of America

First Edition: December 1988

Chapter One

Nina McFall hesitated when she realized the door to her dressing room was open. She knew she hadn't locked it when she ran to get a quick bite of lunch at the television studio's commissary, but she distinctly remembered *shutting* the door. Now it was a few inches ajar. The overhead light had been on when she left, but the room was definitely dark now.

It was just shy of noon. Most of Nina's fellow *Turning Seasons* cast members were out lunching, some of them with their scene partners, going over last-minute line changes before the big 12:30 run-through for the techies. Nina had declined several offers to go to Corrigan's Pub, around the corner from the studio, so she could be alone and concentrate on a killer monologue she was to deliver in today's final scene of the show. Monologues were rare in soap opera scripts, especially half-hour productions like *The Turning Seasons*. Today, however, Nina's character, Melanie Prescott, had a regular diatribe. It was to be the dramatic kiss-off to a more-than-casual romance which would emotionally catapult Melanie

1

into her new story line . . . whatever that was going to be.

Nina glanced up and down the corridor, hoping to see a familiar face approaching. No one was coming. She listened. There were no sounds at either end of the hall or from inside any of the other dressing rooms. She heard nothing but the gentle buzz of the fluorescent ceiling tubes.

She didn't know why she was nervous. Yes, there had been a few incidents of violated privacy and dressing-room burglary lately, but that had all stopped several weeks ago. Besides, Nina kept her cash and credit cards with her now, even when in costume, and there was nothing else of any real value inside. Surely there would be no one inside with the lights off. Or would there?

You're just being silly, she told herself. One too many "partnerships" with handsome NYPD Detective Lieutenant Dino Rossi, involving everything from murder to *more* murder, is making you oversensitive and suspicious of inconsequential things.

Murder. How many had there been since Morty Meyer, owner of Meyer Studios and creator of *The Turning Seasons*, had been poisoned at his and his wife Helen's anniversary party at Leatherwing? Far too many. And Nina had been right there in the thick of things each time. Poor May Minton, respected star of stage and screen, edged off the comeback trail by a blow to the head; Terri Triano and Milly Gowan, the would-be starlets, drugged and strangled, respectively; and then there was . . .

Stop it! Nina told herself. This is all just too morbid! Still, Nina had never shied away from plunging right in and taking charge, electing herself in-house detective and never giving up until the guilty party was exposed and brought to justice—with Dino's help, of course . . . then again, sometimes without it. And often, because of her tenacity and

2

dead-on instincts, she became the murderer's next target. She'd been bound and gagged, shot at, run off the road by automobiles, but so far her lucky star had never dimmed. How long could she expect luck to be on her side? Dino was constantly warning her against taking unnecessary risks and holding back important information. Every time, after the fact, she promised she would never do it again, but she always did. And Dino always forgave her and comforted her as only his strong arms and tender lips could.

Romantic thoughts of Dino brought a flood of emotions Nina had neither the time nor energy to deal with right then. That monologue was waiting to be tackled and tamed once and for all. Shaking off her needless trepidations, she pushed open the door and flicked on the light switch.

Nina let out a small gasp when she saw the wedding gown.

It was draped over the small divan she kept in her dressing room for moments of relaxation. One sleeve of the dress was angled, casually thrown back over the empty space where the bride's head should have been; the other sleeve was demurely positioned across the bodice. The headdress, a riot of seed pearls and silk tulle, crowned the missing face and flowed backward, up and over the couch's arm. The skirt of the dress, like a wave dripping lace and pearls, splashed itself across the rest of the seat, its hem just kissing the floor.

Against the sofa's dark maroon brocade, the overall effect was startling, dramatic—and a bit unsettling. The image of a beleaguered Victorian bride flashed through Nina's mind as she moved forward for a closer inspection.

The gown was apparently an authentic period piece. A spider web of lace and dewy pearls covered the high collar and shoulders of the bodice. The puffed sleeves were also decorated with pearls and

3

lace. Nina gingerly caressed the satin skirt and let her fingers trace the texture of the intricately-constructed body of the dress, which she noticed was dotted with iridescent sequins. All the lace had been dyed and broken down so as to look antique—unless, of course, it really was.

Nina realized she was holding her breath, awed by the beauty of the gown. She slowly stepped back, taking it in from a wider angle. She stood in silent reverie, as if fearing a sudden move or noise would break the spell the dress and setting seemed to create.

Nina was suddenly reminded of her childhood in Madison, Wisconsin. Faded tableaux of youth passed in and out of her consciousness like mixed aromas rising from an old trunk, some stale, some sweet. One stood out above the rest. . . .

Nina was six. She was going to a birthday party, and her mother had insisted she show her new party dress to her father. It was Sunday. Dad was home. That in itself was a celebration of sorts, as his medical practice often kept him away from the family. Nina hated that dress. It was pink dotted swiss. Even though she was only six, she had a sixth sense that told her she would look terrible in that dress with all her red hair and freckles, but her mother insisted she'd be the belle of the ball. Nina's mother sent her downstairs to her father, who was out in the backyard. Passing through the kitchen in her brand-new patent-leather Mary Janes, she noticed a steaming bowl on the countertop. Above her reach, it gave off an irresistible smell, and Nina just *had* to know what was inside. She reached. The shiny soles of her shoes slipped. For support, she grabbed the first thing her fingers brushed—the bowl, which was quickly emptied of fresh chocolate pudding.

Her father heard the crash and came in, finding Nina unharmed, her cotton-candy dress frosted with chocolate, her face streaming with tears. After ten-

4

derly drying the tears, and some chocolate, from her face, he gave her a firm but gentle reprimand and sent her back to her mother, who cleaned her up and laid out an older, but more likable outfit.

Sitting in a chair in her room, afraid that a passing dust mote might mar her appearance and incur her parents' displeasure, Nina waited until it was time to leave. Her mother came to her with an old photo album. Nina remembered smiling at the pictures of her mother as a little girl as she flipped the worn pages back through the years. Nina's mother paused over one page in particular. It was Nina's grandmother in her wedding gown. Nina was awed. It was the most beautiful dress she had ever seen. And to Nina's surprise, her mother said she still had the dress upstairs in Gramma's trunk; one day it would be Nina's, to wear at her own wedding. Little Nina giggled in pleasure.

Then the lesson came. (There was always a lesson when her mother went out of the way to show Nina something.) The dress in the trunk was almost fifty years old and still looked new. Nina's mother pointed out that if she and Gramma had been able to keep it that long in such good condition, Nina could manage to keep her own clothes clean and orderly, at least for a day at a time. Nina nodded and promised she would, wondering how she could *ever* keep such a promise!

She let the memory slip away slowly, savoring its lingering presence. Then her attention was brought back to the carefully arranged gown, and its beauty struck her all over again. She stared at it, bemused.

"Apparently my impromptu staging received exactly the reaction I intended!"

Nina jumped at the intrusion of the male voice and whirled around to see Jason Barnes, the TTS costume designer. He was a bear of a man, filling the doorway with his massive height and shoulder width. It was hard to believe this giant, albeit the gentle one that he was, could possess such incredible feminine instinct and sensitivity to detail in fashion. But he did, and his winning last year's Daytime TV Emmy Award for costume design proved it. He was just over fifty, but could easily pass for ten years younger, with his shock of wavy brown hair that overwhelmed the meager strands of gray. His smile could melt bricks. His eyes, however, were what Nina adored—pale blue with a constant sparkle of mischief. Right now they were fairly dancing with glee.

"I'm sorry I startled you," he said.

"*You* arranged all this?" Nina asked.

"Who else would present your new costume with such mystery and flair?" His voice dropped to a husky whisper.

Nina thought to herself, what a waste that this man has never been on camera! She glanced at the dress again, Jason's words suddenly sinking in. "*I'm* going to wear this?" she asked.

Jason nodded, eyes twinkling, then a look of concern clouded his face. "Don't you like it?"

"Of course I do. Who wouldn't?" Nina carefully picked up the headpiece as if it were made of spun glass. "It's . . . it's breathtaking!"

"Fabulous!" Jason exclaimed. He grinned like a schoolboy showing off an A on his report card. "I spent a lot of quality time on this creation. There are twenty-one yards of silk satin and thirty-two yards of lace in this beauty, not to mention a few bushels of pearls and sequins. We're still working on the shoes. You'll have antique-colored lace slippers with a satin heel. I just want you to remember the feelings you experienced when you first saw the gown. You'll be repeating them on camera in a week or two."

Nina looked at him, cocked her head inquisitively, then smiled and took his hand. "Tell me more," she said in her most coaxing voice.

"Sorry, doll, no can do."

"Jason Barnes, that's not fair!" Nina withdrew her hand from his and took a firm but playful stance. "You know Helen Meyer, our despotic Queen Bee, won't breathe a word of story line to us mere drones, and she's sewn all the writers' mouths shut as well."

"Come on, Nina," Jason said with a laugh. "I only know what's going to happen because I *have* to. Besides, it's more fun for you this way, and you know it."

Nina was about to back down, realizing that Jason had been sworn to secrecy. But she just couldn't let the subject drop, so she tried again. Green eyes sparkling through thick lashes, she purred, "Can't you give me just one little clue for old times' sake?"

Jason responded in mock resignation. "Okay, Nina. How much do you know already?"

"That I'm kissing off my present liaison with the wounded Good Guy and heading off for greener pastures."

"I wouldn't exactly call the landscape greener. If anything, it's . . ."

"What?" Nina pressed.

"Shady," Jason finally said, after careful deliberation.

Nina frowned. "Shady as in dishonest or shady as in cool, green lawns and rose-covered gazebos?"

"I think the *Webster's* Dictionary definition would be a couple of lines down from that, something like, 'Shady: Of darkness, secrecy or concealment.'"

"Hardly seems the appropriate atmosphere for a wedding dress," Nina said, hoping for more.

"I'll tell you two things, for old times' sake—and God help me if Helen finds out. One, it's going to be fun. And two, it's Gothic."

"Gothic?" Nina repeated. She envisioned wind-blown cliffs, a gabled mansion with a single ghostly light beckoning through the fog, and a cloaked

7

woman stealing down a marble staircase as a phantom breeze suddenly blew out the flame of her candle. It sounded like a fun departure from all the tortured realism of corporate backstabbing and indiscreet bed-hopping. Besides, it would be a story that Nina thought would have broad appeal to the younger audience. It would also be something different for *her* to play. She apologized to Jason for being pushy, promising him he hadn't ruined anything but instead had given her something exciting to look forward to.

"Just remember, you didn't hear it from me!"

"I swear I won't say a word, Jason, and I promise I won't try to pry anything else out of you . . . even though I'm very good at it."

"So I've heard," Jason remarked. "At least you're up front about it, unlike some people I could mention."

"You couldn't possibly mean Angela Dolan, now could you, Jason?" Jason smiled noncommittally. "Just as long as there's no comparison. Maybe I've been playing too many scenes with her lately."

Jason rolled his eyes. "You couldn't be like Angela if you tried, thank God! If I had designed this gown for *her*, she'd already be demanding alterations and throwing poison-tipped threats to get the entire story out of me."

Nina laughed, thinking how well Jason knew the temperamental Angela—but then everyone did. Angela had preceded Nina on TTS by several years and considered herself the major reason for the show's continued success. But occasionally Nina would catch Angela mentally comparing the stacks of Nina's fan mail to her own whenever she was in Nina's dressing room. Darling, envious Angela. She *was* very talented, but like many gifted performers, Angela concealed tender layers of insecurity right beneath the bravado.

"Now you try this on when you get a chance," Jason said. "I used the same measurements from the last wedding dress we made for Melanie." Again he twinkled, knowing Melanie Prescott went through men and marriage plans like Kleenex. Still, Nina managed to pull the character off in such a way that she received much genuine sympathy from the TTS viewers.

Nina had to chuckle. "Only in a soap opera can a woman be set up for so much nuptial bliss and yet enjoy so little."

Jason laughed and tenderly scooped the gown off the couch as if it contained an unconscious maiden. "I think our languid beauty has had enough rest. Let's *hang* her, shall we?" Nina gave him a look, surprised by the malicious double meaning with which Jason had delivered that last statement. True, Jason *was* campy, and as comfortable as Nina was with him, she suddenly wondered what he would be capable of if anyone ever made him really angry.

While helping Jason put the dress on a padded hanger, she heard Horst Krueger, the show's top-dog producer, bellow Angela's name down the hall. After several loud goose steps, he made a brusque appearance in Nina's dressing room and demanded to know if either of them had seen "Ms. Dolan." Nina felt trouble brewing in the wings. Horst had been on Angela's case all morning, nitpicking every scene she was in, accusing her of flubbing lines and not taking anything seriously. Horst and Angela had been sort of an "item" for a while, but in the last few weeks there had been a visible frost manteling their exchanges. It was no secret to anyone on the TTS set that there was trouble in paradise.

"Angela's probably at lunch," Nina said.

"I expressly told her to hold off going to lunch until we'd ironed out the changes we have to make in her first scene with Tom Bell. It's just not working."

9

From his tone, Nina gathered he was implying that Angela was the reason it wasn't working. Horst was generally an easygoing man. In his late forties, he still cut an impressive figure: Thinning blond hair set off his chiseled Teutonic features. He commanded a certain paternal respect from the TTS family. Right now, however, he looked like some avenging warrior from a Wagnerian opera, thunder and lightning flashing from his storm-clouded eyes.

"I saw her in Bellamy Carter's office about ten minutes ago," Jason said.

"Were they going over director's notes?" Horst asked.

"No," Jason replied, almost meekly. "Angela was alone and on the phone. When she saw me pass by, she closed the door."

Horst exploded. "What the hell is wrong with that woman? She knows the policy about making personal calls on office phones. She's been on the phone more today than she's been on cue!"

Nina tried to smooth things over. "Horst, you know she's been involved in getting that town house she bought in order. Maybe it was an emergency. Maybe she had to go over there. Believe me, I know how it is—I sweat bullets over the move to my penthouse apartment."

"I don't care if she's redecorating the White House!" he roared. "She's supposed to be a professional, and that means business first. Besides," he added, "the house is finished. She moved in over a week ago."

"Have you seen it?" Jason asked. "Obviously, she's put a lot of work and money into it. She's been . . ."

Horst cut Jason off angrily. "No, I haven't seen it, and I don't care to. If Angela deems it appropriate to bless us with her presence in the next few minutes, tell her I want to see her." He turned on a heavy heel and walked out, slamming the door behind him.

"Whew!" Jason said. "I don't envy Angela when she *does* come back. That man is angrier than I've ever seen him." Nina agreed silently, wondering exactly what Horst was really upset about—or *whom*. This wasn't the first time Angela had taken a cavalier approach to the show, but she was certainly professional enough to handle any kind of changes with ease, mandatory outbursts and temper tantrums on her part aside. Something was up.

Before Nina could think about it further, there was a light knock and Dennis Dale, one of the men from the props department, poked his head in the door. Dennis was a slight but handsome young man in his early twenties. Boyish and bubbly, his mundane task of searching for the usual and often unusual items needed to further the plot or an action never dampened his enthusiasm. He saw his job as an ongoing hunt for buried treasure. Nina didn't know too much about his background, but his engaging and sometimes naive persona made him a favorite around the studio.

He greeted Nina quickly, then spoke to Jason directly, his voice feverish with excitement. "I found it!"

"Did Jerry down in props see it?" Jason asked Dennis.

"No. I wanted you to be the first. I practically ran all the way here." Dennis started fumbling in the pocket of his peacoat. Nina noticed his cheeks were flushed. She couldn't tell if that was due to his exhilaration or the cold weather.

"Should I be in on this or not?" Nina asked.

Jason turned to her. "You've already seen the dress—you might as well see what goes with it."

"I can't imagine anything else going with that gown. It's perfect the way it is."

"I designed it with a high collar for a purpose, Nina," Jason said. "And glad as I am that you like the dress, what Dennis may or may not have found is the real focal point of your new story. You'll be wearing it often."

Nina, her curiosity at fever pitch, moved closer to the two men as Dennis carefully withdrew a small object wrapped in wrinkled tissue paper.

"I found it totally by accident," he crowed. "The whole department has been looking all over the place ever since the edict came down from Helen and the writers. We found some pieces, but so far none of them has passed inspection. I was walking down Ninth Avenue on my lunch break, and I saw this great sconce that I've been wanting to get for my apartment in the window of this dirty secondhand store. So I went in, and there *it* was, right smack in the middle of a display case!"

"Let's see it," Jason said.

But Dennis refrained from unwrapping his prize and continued, his effervescence building with each word until his voice cracked. "I couldn't believe the luck. It was just sitting there. At first I was afraid to even ask how much it was. . . ."

"Open the package, Dennis," Jason said.

". . . I never thought in a million years we'd be so lucky. How much do you think, Jason? How much?"

"I won't know until you open the damn thing!" Jason retorted with some annoyance.

Dennis looked hurt for a minute. Nina noticed. It was clear that Dennis had a critical case of hero worship when it came to Jason. That's why he wanted Jason to see whatever it was first.

Finally, Dennis unfolded the tissue and placed something flat on the palm of his hand that only Jason could see. Jason studied the object for a moment.

"Twenty bucks, Jason, honest. Can you *believe* it?

Twenty bucks! It's probably worth at least *fifty*! All we have to do is clean it up some."

Suddenly a grin spread across Jason's face, and he clapped Dennis on the back so hard Nina thought the young man might collapse. "You done good, kid. It's perfect. I don't care what Helen or the writers say. It's just what *I've* been looking for."

Dennis beamed. Nina tried to sneak a peek at the mystery item, but Jason was caught up in Dennis's earlier enthusiasm and started leading him out of the room, talking with great animation, one arm wrapped around the young man's shoulder. They looked like two members of a team that had just won the pennant. Feeling forgotten and ignored, Nina cleared her throat loudly. They turned and looked at her as if they'd never seen her before.

"May I remind you two *adolescents* that this *is* my dressing room? That I have a helluva day ahead of me yet? That I have lines to memorize? Would it be *too* much to ask to *see* what this *thing* is? After all, if I'm the one who has to wear it, maybe it should have *my* approval before we roll out the barrel, eh boys? Please?"

Dennis and Jason looked at each other, then broke out in guffaws. Nina just stared at them icily. "Of course you can see it, doll," Jason said contritely. "I'm sorry. It's just that we've been looking all over town for the right piece, and . . ."

"Dennis," Nina interrupted, "let me see what you have in your hand before you both drive me *crazy*!"

All smiles, Dennis came over to Nina and dramatically displayed what he held. Nestled in his palm was a brooch unlike any Nina had ever seen. Obviously a cast-off costume piece, judging from the price Dennis paid for it, it was still strangely magnificent. Its center was composed of three rubylike stones in a faux gold setting. Around it, several pieces of what looked like onyx or black glass fanned out in a circular pattern. Rhinestones glittered here and there like drops of dew.

"So, what do you think?" asked Jason. Nina looked up at their smiling faces, then down again at the brooch. She could neither comprehend nor describe the odd sensation that seemed to crawl down her spine. Her eyes kept being drawn to the three red stones. She shivered involuntarily, then hoped that Dennis and Jason hadn't noticed. For some unknown reason, those fake, faceted gems reminded her of drops of blood.

Chapter Two

Several hours later, Nina was once again in her dressing room, another day of triumph and bitter defeat for *The Turning Seasons* cast of characters captured on video tape. Three weeks from now, housewives, college students, and even a surprising number of workaday professionals would see Melanie Prescott deliver the bone-stinging coup de grace to poor Shane Bancroft. Some of them would applaud, some would write nasty letters, but all of them would tune in the next day to see how Shane and Melanie picked up their lives and went on.

Nina looked at herself in the mirror as she wiped the last vestiges of Melanie's makeup off her face. Nina often thought it a wonder she wasn't schizophrenic, popping in and out of a whole different person's skin five days a week. But that's what acting was all about.

What then, Nina asked herself, was *life* all about? And why was she in this strange, introspective mood? Absently, she turned her head and took in the wedding gown hanging on her costume rack. That's what had done it, that and her mother's promise that Nina would wear Gramma's gown on her own wedding day. Somehow that didn't seem like a plausible possibility at the moment. A husband, children, and all the responsibilities that went with both just didn't fit into Nina's game plan right now. She wondered if they ever would or could. She had a life she knew most people would give an arm for, but sometimes, especially late at night when Dino was busy on a case and she was studying scripts, or sitting over a single, lonely cup of coffee at dawn *still* studying scripts, Nina felt a certain void. There was supposed to be *more*. Her mother had it, or it had always seemed to Nina that she did. Could Dino and his son, Peter, fill that emptiness in her life?

Nina sighed, rose, and began taking off the red siren number she'd worn to lambaste Shane in the final scene of today's episode. Hanging it carefully and making a mental note to return it to wardrobe, she slipped into a pale green silk robe and went back to her dressing table, standing for a moment to take stock of herself in the mirror.

At thirty-four, Nina considered herself just on the verge of her prime. Even after a day like this, even without makeup, she liked what she saw. Her robe was open, revealing that her hectic schedule and carefully planned regimen of diet and exercise still kept her figure supple and curved in all the right places beneath her beige lace bra and panties. Her jade green eyes still sparkled as they had when she was a young girl, and her glorious head of rose-gold hair still glowed without the aid of henna. Even the freckles that dusted her nose didn't detract from the overall picture. They gave her face character. Nina suddenly felt very in touch with who she was and what she wanted. The future seemed crowded with exciting, unknown possibilities, and Nina was ready to enjoy each one of to the fullest. *That* was what life was all about.

With renewed vigor and a contented smile, Nina closed her robe, tied the sash, and began gathering up the discarded facial tissues she'd used to take off her makeup. She stopped, staring at a cluster of them smeared with red lipstick. In their midst, to Nina's astonishment, glittered the brooch. She gingerly brushed the soiled tissues away from the piece of jewelry as if it might bite. She remembered now that on their way out Dennis and Jason had said they were going to show the pin to the production people and to Sally Burman, the writer who was on the floor that day. Dennis had also said he'd return it to Nina's dressing room later so she could put it and the wedding dress on to show Jason.

Nina still couldn't understand the unsettling effect the brooch had on her. There seemed to be a mutual dislike between her and the object. But that was impossible. It was nothing more than a conglomeration of glass and gold plate. Pushing her aversion aside, she picked it up. It was heavy. It was going to be a pain in the neck to wear, but she'd do it.

As she laid the brooch back down on the vanity's surface, there was a brief knock on the door, and she heard Robin Tally's voice calling her name. Nina opened the door with a smile and greeted her friend warmly, then invited her in.

"I'm glad you're still here, Nina," Robin said. "I was just watching the tapes of today's show and I had to tell you how terrific that last scene was that you did with Shane. I've never seen you tear up the scenery with such aplomb."

Nina laughed, feeling a little self-conscious color rise in her cheeks. "Stop, please . . . no, *don't* stop! I love every word!" she kidded. Nina noticed that Robin was still in her costume but had pulled her long black hair up off her neck with a wooden comb.

"I really mean it, Nina," Robin went on. "Everyone in the studio was glued to the monitor—even Angela, though I think I did see her turn several shades of green. She's probably harassing poor Sally Burman right now for equal script time."

"And we all know she'll get it," Nina replied without rancor.

"Has Angela extended her invitation to you yet?"

"What invitation?" Nina asked.

Before Robin could reply, her eyes fell upon the wedding dress, and she let out a gasp. Nina laughed softly. "That was my first reaction, too."

"You'll be stunning in it, Nina! It's a lot more elegant than what I'm wearing to the ball."

"'What ball? Have you been holding out on me?" Nina chided.

"No, no. All I know is that there's this big costume ball coming up to kick off a new story line. I really don't even know which character is throwing it."

"I tried to pry some details out of Jason," Nina said, "but I didn't get very far. Now what's this about an invitation from Angela?"

"I know more about the new story line than I do about that," Robin said with a laugh. "She just pulled me aside on the set today and told me to keep tonight free for something *very special*, and she'd talk to me before we both left, and don't tell anybody."

"Which you just did," Nina remarked.

"I have no secrets from my best friend. Too bad it doesn't work both ways," Robin added, feigning irritation.

"What does that mean?" Nina asked in surprise.

"It means, after all this time, I think there's quite a lot more going on between you and the dangerously delicious Detective Rossi than you're telling me."

"Maybe not quite so much as you think—or as much as we'd *both* like to imagine," Nina said a little ruefully.

"And how do you feel about that?" Robin pressed.

"There are some . . . feelings . . . a woman just doesn't talk about, especially when she doesn't fully understand them herself—even if it irks her best friend. Sometimes things are better left uninvestigated."

"That's funny," Robin said, "coming from *you*, of all people!" Nina said nothing. Robin went over to examine the wedding gown, then turned back to Nina. "I wonder what Dino would say if he saw you in this?"

"Unless he watches the show faithfully," Nina said, ignoring the implications, "and we know he doesn't, he never will. Subject closed?" Robin tactfully pretended to be absorbed in looking at the dress while Nina thought about Dino. The most recent mélange of mayhem and murder that had reared its ugly head among the TTS cast had almost cost Dino his life. A crazed fan, neurotically blending fact and fiction, had declared himself Nina's "Secret Lover," and after doing away with Nina's onscreen romantic interest, he had finally targeted Dino as his true rival.

Nina had never been so scared in her life. Yes, it had been murder that brought Dino and Nina together in the first place, but for the first time it really hit Nina that it could also separate them forever. Ever since that episode, Nina had found herself, unconsciously at first, then deliberately, holding back with her law-enforcing lover. She tried to tell herself that it was his job and that she too took dangerous risks that could also terminate their relationship—and their lives. The only difference was, Nina could stop getting involved and keep herself out of danger. Dino couldn't and wouldn't. He loved what he did too much, and if push came to shove, Nina knew which commitment Dino would choose if she forced the issue. Either way, Nina could lose him. She wedged

19

the thought into the back of her mind and asked Robin if she was leaving soon.

"No, Rafe and I have to pretape a couple of scenes because they don't have room to use the restaurant set again tomorrow. We'll probably be here a couple more hours."

"That shouldn't be too trying, knowing how you and Rafe feel about each other."

Robin bit her lip before speaking. "I'm not sure we do."

Nina looked surprised. "Don't tell me you two are on the outs again?"

"Yes. No. Well, maybe."

"That's clear," Nina joked. Then she grew serious and put a comforting hand on Robin's arm. "What's wrong now?"

"I think maybe Rafe and I feel trapped. Maybe we need some space—freedom to see other people."

"Is that what you really want, honey?" Nina asked. Robin looked away. Nina moved to face her. "Are you trying to tell me there's somebody else? In *your* life, I mean."

"I'm not clamming up on you or anything, Nina," Robin said, on the verge of tears, "but like you just said, some feelings a woman just has to keep to herself."

All of this sounded serious to Nina, who had watched Rafe and Robin fall in and out of love and lust for a long time. But her romantic soul told her that these two really did belong together. She knew the tensions an "in-show" romance could create, and a double-career romance wasn't exactly in any couple's favor, either. While Nina mused how that fact echoed the difficulties between her and Dino, Robin discovered the brooch.

"That goes with the wedding gown," Nina said. "What do you think of it?"

"It's—well, the only word I can come up with is . . . Gothic."

"Then it's perfect," Nina said without much conviction. "It would probably be worth quite a bit of money if those stones were real."

Just then Angela Dolan appeared in the doorway.

"Knock, knock. Is this a private party, or can anyone join in?"

Nina cast an amused glance at Robin, then invited Angela in. A needless formality, for Angela was already across the room and ogling the wedding gown before the words were spoken.

"It's simply *divine*, Nina, darling," Angela cooed. "Is there some happy occasion coming up in your life that you haven't shared with the rest of us?"

Nina rolled her eyes. Angela never changed. The harmless rivalry that existed between the two women was infamous around the TTS set. Most people enjoyed it. Nina had to admit she did, too. "It's just a costume, Angela. But I'm surprised you like it. Victorian really isn't your style."

"*Au contraire*," Angela said, a little miffed. "Victoriana is the epitome of PGR."

Robin and Nina exchanged confused glances.

"What's PGR?" Robin asked, taking the bait.

"Passion, glamour, romance . . . the divine sparks of life, of course! The things that count!"

Robin checked her watch. "I should get back on the set soon for those pretapes. I just have to fix my hair a little." She started out.

"Robin," said Angela, stopping her in mid-step. "In case I don't see you before we leave, I want you to be sure and take this." She reached into the pocket of her lavender gabardine suit and took out a small business card. "Here," she said, extending the card to Robin. "This is where I'll be meeting you and Nina tonight."

Robin took the card as Nina said, "Excuse me, Angela, but meeting you where for what?"

Angela turned to face Nina. "Why, I assumed Robin told you. It's girls' night out, just the three of us." Robin looked contrite. "I'm sorry, darling," Angela said to her, "I thought I made it clear to you that the invitation included Nina."

"Yes, you did, but I didn't know any of the details. And now I really have to run." Robin started out the door again.

"I'll see you later, darling. Nine-thirty. Sharp!"

"Yes, Angela," Robin said, "but we—or I, anyway—can't make it too late tonight. I don't have too heavy a day tomorrow, but . . ."

"I understand perfectly," Angela interrupted. "We all need our beauty sleep, but now and again it doesn't hurt to kick up our heels. It'll just be a quick couple of drinks, I promise."

Robin nodded, then told Nina she'd call her later. Nina turned and saw Angela's eyes sweeping the room like a crow looking for sparkling baubles to take to its nest. It was inevitable that the brooch would catch her eye. By the time Nina joined her at the dressing table, Angela was holding it up to the light.

"Exquisite," Angela pronounced. "Fake, but exquisite. Is it from a personal collection?" Nina ignored the barb. "That was a joke, darling!" Angela tittered, and Nina looked at her more closely. A certain glow Nina hadn't noticed before seemed to be emanating from her.

"The brooch is a prop, Angela. It goes with the gown."

"Well, it looks like you have a very interesting story line on the horizon. And not a moment too soon, after that onscreen eruption today with poor Shane. Maybe he'll get thrown *my* way. I wouldn't mind acting with him. I don't think he usually knows what he's doing, but he did have one or two very nice, honest moments today. But then so did you. Really! I don't think people around here give you *half* the respect you deserve as an actress."

"Thank you, Angela," Nina said, trying not to show how dumbfounded she was by Angela's uncharacteristic praise. She retrieved the brooch from Angela's grasp and put it back on the table. "Now what *is* all this tonight?"

"I've always loved rubies," Angela mused. "Even fake ones. They're so full of . . ." Angela stopped, trying to find the right words.

"So full of PGR?" Nina suggested.

"Precisely!" Angela replied. "Red roses, red wine, red jewels . . . they all have a certain inherent— *passion*, don't you think?"

Nina glanced at the brooch and frowned. Again, the only image that flickered in her mind was blood. She looked away, focusing once more on Angela, who was still looking covetously at the pin. "About tonight, Angela. What *is* it?"

"Oh, tonight. Well, it's nothing *too* special. . . ."

"Then why the secrecy? Why Robin and me?"

"It's no secret. Well, yes it is. And it *is* special, but I only want to share it with the two of you."

"Why?" Nina persisted.

"Because . . . everything aside, I feel a certain kinship with the two of you." Angela ignored Nina's amazed look and went on with as much genuine feeling as Nina thought she possessed. "We've shared a lot. This business isn't easy for a woman— or a man, for that matter. We're so much . . . *product* . . . rolling off a conveyor belt in here, day in and day out. We tend to lose sight of things like love and friendship for each other. The things that really *count*."

Nina couldn't resist. "What about passion, glamour, and romance?"

"Darling, be serious," Angela scolded. "We're at a

time in our lives when *some* of those things must take a backseat. Within reach of course, but still a backseat. Now, please, for me, say you'll come tonight? I promise I'll explain everything when we all meet."

"All right," Nina said with a sigh. "I know it's supposed to be at nine-thirty, but I don't know where."

Angela clasped Nina's hands. "Thank you! I'll just jot the address down. You'll simply *adore* this place." Angela looked around, then went over to Nina's miniature writing desk and swept a few fan letters aside. "There seems to be enough room here to write," she said with emphasis as she grabbed a pen and ripped off a small portion of Nina's personal stationery. Nina prayed for patience as she waited for Angela to write down the information. "Here," she said, thrusting the paper into Nina's hands.

Nina looked at the card. "Jule's?" she asked. "I've never heard of it."

"It's *the* new in place. I've been there once or twice and always leave just craving for more." Angela giggled again, then blushed, as if remembering an off-color joke. For a moment, Nina wondered if Angela had indulged in a liquid lunch, but she smelled no alcohol on her breath.

"Are we playing dress-up tonight, or is it casual?" Nina asked.

Angela thought before answering. "Wear something chic, but sincere. Borrow something from wardrobe if you have to. I do it all the time. Jason's a doll about that sort of thing as long as you return the clothes in one piece."

Memories of pink dotted swiss and chocolate pudding crossed Nina's mind. I'd better wear something of my own, she decided. When next Nina looked, Angela was fingering the brooch again.

"Do you know what's going on with Tom Bell?" Angela asked out of the blue.

24

"Why?" Nina replied, throwing the question back, hoping for some more to go on.

"He's been having difficulty on the set lately. I noticed it in particular today in his scenes with me."

I'm not surprised, Nina thought to herself, the way you ad-lib lines and change blocking, not to mention the total intent of the scene at times. Everyone had difficulty doing scenes with her. Yet part of what Angela was saying was true. Nina *had* noticed that Tom was off lately. He'd been on the show for several years, playing the same smarmy business executive. Usually he was very happy-go-lucky out of character, but recently his usual verve seemed somewhat diminished. And, too, there was that problem today that Horst put Angela at the center of, not Tom.

"I think he has romantic troubles," Angela confided.

"What makes you think that?"

Angela absently polished one of the red stones with the tip of her finger. "I can't *tell* you how stunning this would look on what I'm planning to wear tonight . . . after a good cleaning, of course."

Again, Nina retrieved the brooch. "What makes you think Tom's having romantic troubles?"

"Oh, well, he's just exhibiting all the signs. Preoccupation. No appetite. Irritability. And he's got bags under his eyes that only result from mooning over unrequited love."

"Angela, I think you're making a little too much of this."

"Think what you like—but I *did* see Tom creeping out of Robin's dressing room just before our final taping. He looked . . . defeated."

Nina immediately dismissed the whole idea. Yes, Tom was attractive, but nothing to compare with Rafe. "I'm sure there's a logical explanation," she said firmly.

"Fine," Angela retorted, dismissing the subject. "I

25

was just curious. But whatever is troubling him, it's starting to affect his work, and that means it's affecting mine as well. Aside from lunch, it's been a bitch of a day." Angela dramatically swept a few stray wisps of silver-blond hair off her forehead.

"Did you and Horst—er—get everything squared away this afternoon?" Nina asked delicately. She already knew the answer but was fishing for some explanations.

"Of course. I already told you the dynamics of my scenes today weren't working because of Tom, not me. Horst just wanted to flex his muscles for Helen's benefit—she was up in the booth this morning watching the rehearsals. It was a childish way to draw attention to himself and reinforce his status with the Powers That Be. I can't speak for Helen, but I wasn't impressed. Whatever his problem is, he'll get over it. He'll have to," she added airily. Nina decided to change subjects.

"I hear you've moved into your new town house."

"Yes, I have, darling, and it's just New York splendor personified. I can't wait to have an official housewarming. It *was* a big financial step for me to make, but I decided I deserve it. What good is money if you can't spend it on things that make you happy? What's life if you don't *live* it?" Again, Nina noticed that Angela was glowing, and Nina had the feeling there was more behind it than a new place to hang her hat. More likely, Nina guessed, there was a new man in her life, which meant Horst had probably gotten the boot.

There was a knock at the door. Grand Central Station, Nina thought. "Come in," she called. The door opened, and Horst moved in with purposeful steps.

"I'm glad you're still here, Angela," he said grimly.

"Why?" Angela asked with a definite edge.

"We have to do an insert. We just noticed there

was a boom shadow in the background when you delivered your last line on Tom's exit and . . ."

Angela flared. "*We* just noticed, or *you* just noticed? Or did you just *ignore* it on purpose when the scene was done so you could deliberately hold me hostage in this place after hours?"

"I'd have no reason to do that, Angela," Horst said uncomfortably, stealing a glance at Nina. "No reason at all."

"Then you're either being vindictive or you're not doing your job," Angela snapped. "This is inexcusable!"

"Come on, Angela," Nina said lightly. "It happens."

"Well, it shouldn't," Angela retorted.

"The longer you complain," Horst said, lowering his voice to a threatening tone, "the longer you'll be here. Personally, I don't care. I've got all night." There was a tense silence as Horst and Angela faced off. The moment was broken by Dennis, who stuck his head in the door with his usual smile.

"Hi, Miss Dolan, Mr. Krueger. Nina, Jason asked me to come up and see if you're ready to try on the dress so he could see it."

"Just about, Dennis. I've had *several* visitors."

"Okay. Oh, Miss Dolan? There's a delivery for you at the front desk. Looks like roses. Long stemmed."

Angela beamed. Horst glowered. Nina just wanted them all to leave.

"I'll see to them immediately," Angela purred. She looked directly at Horst. "*Then* I'll come down to the floor and help 'patch up' today's show." A momentary look of pain and defeat washed over Horst's face, and then he simply and silently left.

Angela cast one more furtive glance at the brooch, then bid Nina a mellow good-bye and moved to the door. "I'll see you later then, darling?"

"Yes, Angela. I'll be there."

"Wonderful! I promise you you won't be disappointed. I realize it was rather presumptuous of me not to even *ask* if you had other plans tonight, but . . ."

"It's all right, Angela," Nina said. "I don't."

"Good. And Dennis, be a dear and walk out front with me. There's something I'd like to ask you." She turned back to Nina. "Ta, darling." Angela swept out with Dennis in tow, and Nina closed and locked the door with a sigh of relief.

She went back to the dressing table and sat down heavily. So much went on behind the scenes. Sometimes she wondered what the fans would think if they only knew. Her mind drifted to what Angela had said about Tom Bell and Robin. Under other circumstances, Nina would have quickly put such thoughts out of her mind, but after the conversation Nina had just had with Robin . . . Well, I'm not going to pry, Nina promised herself. If there's anything between Robin and Tom, that's their business. And if there *isn't* anything between Horst and Angela anymore, that's not my business, either.

Nina concentrated on finishing cleaning up and trying on the gown. The reflection of the brooch in the mirror caught her eye. She'd have to wear that, too. She picked it up and fiddled with the catch on the back. It was stiff with age, but she managed to force it open. Suddenly it slipped from her grasp and Nina grabbed for it. Then she winced in pain and let the brooch fall into her lap. Somehow she'd pricked her thumb.

She sucked on the wound immediately, then looked closely at her thumb. A small drop of blood oozed from the tiny perforation. Nina stared at it, realizing that her initial image of the red stones in the brooch had been correct. They *were* the color of fresh blood, and the pin had just drawn the first drop.

Chapter Three

Nina and Robin shivered in the taxi as it turned onto Amsterdam Avenue and headed uptown. The driver obviously didn't have the heat on high, so Nina pulled the collar of her leather trench coat up around her face until she could feel the warm fur trim. Then she snuggled down into the seat, searching for warmth.

Nina had picked up Robin at her apartment, and after a few words about Robin's pretape session and Nina's fitting for the wedding gown, the conversation had lapsed into that comfortable silence that only exists between two close friends.

Robin was looking out the window, engaged in people watching. Traffic was unusually heavy for this time on a Thursday night, and Nina noticed that the driver smiled every time they stopped for a red light and the meter clicked an additional fifteen cents for every eighth mile. Robin caught Nina's gaze and smiled.

"Not too many people on foot tonight," Robin commented.

"I'm not surprised," Nina said. "March came in like a lion, and it's still roaring." The driver mumbled something that Nina could not for the life of her understand. She checked his prominently displayed identification. Amir Ben Kassimer. That explained it. Nina wondered how much English he knew besides street addresses and denominations of American currency. She decided it didn't matter as long as he got them where they were going.

She was beginning to regret that she'd agreed to Angela's "girls' night out." It would have been a perfect opportunity to curl up in her lovely penthouse with a good book, a snifter of brandy, and her feline roommate, Chessy. She'd already memorized her lines for Friday's taping; she had a light day, only two scenes. There was a message on her phone machine from Dino when she got home from work. After feeding Chessy and giving him a good dose of love and affection, she returned Dino's call, glad for the chance to touch base with him. It turned out to be a strange conversation—full of undercurrents, but superficial.

Dino apologized for not having been in touch; he'd been up to his ears in a heavy case that was just wrapping up. Nina was pleased when he said it probably took him longer than usual because she hadn't been involved. Nina said she hoped they could get together soon, and Dino said he did, too, but tonight he had tickets to take his son, Peter, to a hockey game. Annoyed that it had apparently never occurred to him that she might like to go with them, Nina coolly wished him a good time with his son and said she had plans of her own. Dino said okay, he'd talk to her soon, and that was that.

His lack of interest concerning Nina's plans bothered her. She'd never considered jealousy an attractive trait in a man, but still, a little curiosity would have been flattering as well as comforting.

Even though she realized that Dino knew she needed a little space and was merely giving it to her, that space was beginning to seem like a deep pit of self-indulgent introspection and loneliness.

"Do you know anything about this place we're going to?" Robin asked, interrupting Nina's thoughts.

"Not a thing, except that in Angela's words, it's '*the* new in place.' I still can't get over the fact that she asked us out for . . . whatever."

"I think she's lonely," Robin offered. "She really doesn't have any close friends that I know of, except her cats. Maybe she's mellowing with age or turning over a new leaf or something."

You wouldn't think so, honey, Nina thought to herself, if you heard what she was implying about you and Tom Bell. Nina was tempted to throw out a casual question about Rafe but thought better of it. She decided there must be a full moon or something. Rafe and Robin. Horst and Angela. Nina and Dino— there were definitely some external disruptive forces at work against Cupid.

"I'd say it's pretty much over between Angela and Horst," Robin said, as if reading her thoughts.

"Why?"

"The two of them had a shouting match in the studio after they thought everybody was gone. Rafe and I were on the way out and we could hear their voices all the way into the hall. It was pretty nasty."

Nina groaned inwardly. God knows what kind of mood Angela would be in tonight, and when Horst was uptight and irritable, he took it out on everybody in the cast.

"Let's just hope it blows over," she said. "The show's hard enough to do when everybody's happy— although I can't remember exactly the last time that was!"

"We're here," Robin announced as the cab pulled over to the curb. "And there's a line to get in!"

Nina paid and tipped the driver, then followed Robin out into the street. They were on the Upper West Side, near Columbia University. A mixed bag of a neighborhood—you could eat an elegant meal, buy some of the purest cocaine, or lose your life, all in a matter of a few well-chosen blocks. You just had to know where to go, and where not to go.

A cold wind blasted Nina, swirling refuse around her feet and hurling urban soot and grit into her eyes, as Robin pulled her into the line of eager would-be patrons waiting to gain entrance.

Nina hardly looked at—or could see, for that matter—the facade of Jule's, an old Manhattan mansion. There was no sign or placard stating they'd come to the right place. Only the address and the restless throng told them they were there.

"Do you see Angela?" Robin asked, peering up ahead at the line.

Nina didn't bother to look. "She'd hardly be waiting out here in this weather."

"Maybe she made reservations or something," Robin suggested, teeth chattering.

"This looks like a private club. You either have to know someone to get in or pave your way with cash."

"So where does that leave us?" Robin asked dubiously.

"Honey," Nina reminded her with a smile, "we're *stars*. Maybe small ones in a big sky, but stars nonetheless. If we get stopped, we'll just play righteous indignation, turn up our noses in total indifference to whoever's boorish and ignorant behavior, and waltz right in."

"What if that doesn't work?" Robin said, now even more dubious.

"Then we'll pay and force Angela to fork over the money later. This *was* her idea." Nina wormed her way through the crowd, Robin following, paying no attention to the disgruntled looks and rude comments that swirled and eddied in their wake. The door to Jule's, a massive piece of oak hung by wrought iron hinges, opened just as Nina reached for the knob. A solid mass of a man barred their way.

"I'm sorry, ladies," he announced with self-important authority, "but we're full up, as you must have seen by the line outside. Those people ain't waitin' for cabs out there, you know." Something about the sound of his voice made Nina hesitate before saying anything. She studied him closely. He wasn't overly tall, but what there was of him was all muscle—except a little around the stomach. A beer-and-barbell type, Nina thought. His blond hair was shoulder length, and some of the ends curled incestuously with his trimmed but heavy beard. His eyes were beady and brown, and not in the least friendly.

"You can't be full already," Nina said sweetly. "It's still early. Besides, we're supposed to meet somebody here."

"I got fire laws to obey. You ever get caught in a stampede of panicked socialites when some drunk decides to have a little fun and yell *fire*? You know the kinda holes four-inch heels can make in your back?"

"No, I can't say that I do," Nina said. "Nor do I want to. But . . ."

"It's not pretty," he said flatly. "Sorry about this, but— Hey! You're Nina McFall, aren't you?"

"Yes, I am," Nina said with a triumphant smile at Robin. "Do you watch *The Turning Seasons*?"

"Not anymore," the man said with a trace of bitterness Nina didn't understand. She also noticed that his flash of recognition hadn't come with the usual warmth or excitement Nina had come to expect. "Come on in," he said grudgingly and stepped back into the shadows of the entry.

Nina frowned. There was definitely something familiar about this man, but she couldn't place him for the life of her. Before Nina could voice any

33

objections, Robin was halfway past her, escaping the cold with relish. Nina had no choice but to follow.

It took several minutes for Nina's eyes to adjust to the dimness. She heard the door shut behind her and turned to find the burly bouncer practically breathing down her neck. Nina shivered, thanked him, and quickly caught up with Robin. They were in a sort of anteroom. Nina could make out what looked like rich walnut paneling on the walls. Voices and music drifted in from behind double doors off to the right. Several indistinguishable couples were mixing in the shadows. Nina saw the bearded man move in front of them and say a few words to another well-muscled "gatekeeper," who was obviously collecting admission money. It was, no doubt, a high tab—a costly but effective way to keep the wrong sort from entering the Emerald City.

Nina and Robin were then surprisingly waved on, cash intact. The bearded man continued to puzzle Nina. She decided to thank him for letting them in and take the opportunity to see if she could figure out where she might know him from. But when she looked back, he was gone. They checked their coats. The double doors were opened for them as if by magic, and the two women entered Manhattan's newest inner sanctum for the chic elite.

Nina and Robin both stood in momentary awe of the beauty of the larger, formal foyer they'd just entered. The crowd noises were louder now, but Nina blocked them out. She felt as if she'd walked into the past.

The hall was huge. Nina's heels clicked across the black-and-white marble-patterned floor as she slowly moved toward a grand, sweeping staircase of pearl gray marble that gracefully uncoiled up to the second floor. To the right, three sets of French doors opened onto an inviting drawing room. To the left, flanked by lush potted palms, rose Palladian windows dressed in the sheerest of white lace curtains, which let in just enough light from the street for ambience, but whose texture did not allow outsiders to see in. Above them a huge crystal chandelier, electrified with flickering candle bulbs, shed a flattering light upon them. Several men and women, some in evening clothes, wandered about, speaking in hushed tones.

"I was beginning to wonder out there," Robin whispered, taking Nina's arm, "if this was going to be worth the trouble. I think it is. It doesn't seem all that crowded, either," she added.

"I'm sure it isn't," Nina said. "It's good marketing strategy to keep people wild with eagerness to get into a club like this. Let's go upstairs."

They made their way up the staircase to the second floor. The marble railing continued around in a circular fashion, almost bending back on itself, and led to a smaller but no less grand stairway leading to a third floor. Nina saw that this was roped off with a thick, red velvet rope, and immediately wondered what was up there. At either end of the balcony were two large archways. Luxuriant red velvet drapes, discreetly parted enough to allow entry and held by gold-tasseled ties, hung in lavish folds. Nina and Robin headed for the nearest set, entering a large, dark room of faded Victorian grandeur. Directly in front of them, and filling half the space, were groupings of faded antique sofas and chairs covered in damask. Running the length of the far-right wall was a worn but rugged mahogany bar, its stools decorated with damask throws. Overlapping Oriental rugs were spread in a confusion of rich color over the polished hardwood floors. Massive, ornate floor-to-ceiling mirrors, their gilded frames beginning to chip and peel, alternated with clusters of old oil paintings that depicted scenes of bygone glory. Gilded sconces adorned the spaces in between. Overhead, ceiling fans lazily stirred the smoky air that was dimly lit by chandeliers of varying age and design. The overall impression was one of elegant decadence—ruined finery stolen from the manor house of some long-dead English lord.

One look at Robin told Nina that her friend shared her excitement and appreciation. There was a good crowd, but the room was not overly full. Robin suggested they look for Angela, and Nina nodded, eager to explore the rest of this wonderful place. They followed the bar to the back of the room, where mismatched antique tables and chairs were set up for dining. On each table was a small Victorian bud vase that held a single red rose. Waiters and waitresses, dressed in red, white, and black, were in the process of serving, and Nina glanced at several tempting trays of food as she made her way to the rear, where a narrow staircase dipped down into an even more dimly lit area. Music vibrated in the shadows. They descended.

Passing through another curtained archway, Nina and Robin found themselves in a room very much like the one above but with more cozy seating arrangements surrounding a large open space filled with dancing patrons. Nina couldn't see a band or disc jockey and guessed the music was piped in through some well-hidden speaker system.

They worked their way around the dance floor to find yet another staircase. They ascended into another room similar to the first, but equipped with a regulation-sized billiard table, several chess setups, a dart board, a vintage player piano, and a small corner bar—a game room, of sorts. Nina and Robin wove through the crowd of talkers, drinkers, and players, on the lookout for Angela. They eventually came full circle, back onto the balcony directly across from the archway they had originally entered when they came up the stairs.

36

"I didn't see Angela anywhere, did you?" Robin asked.

"No, but I was so distracted by everything, I might have missed her. This could go on all night. It's just a little past nine-thirty. Why don't we go to the bar and let *her* find *us*?" Robin agreed, and they crossed the upstairs foyer, went through the drapes again, and settled themselves on two available stools at the bar.

"Good evening, ladies. What can I get for you?"

Nina, who had been watching the entrance when she sat down, turned and looked into the most startling pair of green eyes she had ever seen, her own notwithstanding. The bartender was, she guessed, in his late twenties. A trim, muscular body filled out his crisp white shirt, and tapered to slender hips. His dark brown curly hair tumbled over his forehead like the breaking crest of a wave. Perfect white teeth shone between his full smiling lips. His jaw was square, his chin dimpled. If he were not breathing and talking, he could have been a classic piece of marble, fashioned into a statue of idealized, sensitive virility.

Nina noticed that Robin was so mesmerized by him that she had a hard time ordering her Campari and soda. Nina asked for a vodka gimlet, and with a nod and an even more dazzling smile, he moved down the bar to prepare the drinks.

"Take my word for it," Nina said once he was out of earshot, "if Helen were here, she'd have that young man on her cast list faster than you could say Treat Williams!"

"He's *gorgeous*," Robin said. "Maybe he *is* an actor. Just about every waiter and bartender in this city is."

"Well, if he's not, he should be," Nina remarked. "It looks like Angela's going to be fashionably late, so let's stay here and chat for a while."

37

In a moment the bartender returned with cocktail napkins and their drinks. "First time here?" he asked.

"How did you know?" Nina asked.

"I saw you both when you came in. You didn't just plop down and order a drink. You looked at everything. You came here to see rather than *be* seen."

"Well, you're right," Nina admitted. "My name's Nina, and this is my friend Robin."

"I'm Jay. Nice to meet both of you. You do the place justice."

Nina swore she saw Robin blush. "My friend and I were just wondering," Nina began, "are you an actor?"

"No," Jay said. "Why?"

Nina waited for Robin to say something. She didn't, or couldn't, so Nina continued. "I know a lot of struggling actors, and *established* ones, too, for that matter, who would kill for your looks."

Jay smiled. "Thanks for the compliment, but I'm just a bartender. Never considered being anything else." A shadow briefly passed over Jay's face. His smile faltered for a moment, then resumed. For that moment, Nina thought he looked—haunted. "Are you a producer or something?" he asked. "We get a lot of them in here."

"No. I'm an actress," Nina said. "So is Robin. We're both on the soap opera *The Turning Seasons*."

"That sounds familiar," Jay said. "I don't watch too much television, especially during the day, but I hear it's a pretty hectic job."

"It is," Robin spoke up at last, "but it has its rewards."

"And it can be a lot of fun," Nina added, sipping her drink.

"But not an easy field to break into," Jay said. "And I guess it also takes a lot of guts and talent to stay *in* the field once you've gotten the big break."

"True," said Nina. "But there have been instances

38

where an unknown has been 'discovered' and worked with until he—or she—got rolling."

"Are you offering me a job?" Jay asked abruptly.

Nina was caught off guard by the question. "Well, surely I'm not the first person who's come in here and suggested you give show business a try, am I?"

"No," he said hesitantly. "I've been . . . approached . . . before, but usually the offer has come with a tangle of strings attached. From women *and* men."

"I'm sorry," Nina said sincerely. "I hope you didn't think for one minute that either Robin or I were feeding you some kind of a line."

Jay grinned. "No, I could tell right away you two weren't that type. I hope I haven't embarrassed you or . . ."

"Not at all," Nina assured him. "Robin and I are both happily attached and are staunch believers in old-fashioned monogamy. Right, Robin?" Robin gave a weak smile and nodded. That was a stupid thing to say, Nina realized, considering what Robin had mentioned earlier about herself and Rafe. She quickly changed the subject. "If you like," she said to Jay, "come by Meyer Studios sometime, on West Sixty-sixth Street. I could introduce you to the casting director or the producer, and you could test the waters by being an extra."

"What's an extra?" Jay asked.

"Those people you always see in the background," Robin said. "The restaurant patrons, hospital doctors, and patients. Window dressing, basically."

Before Jay could reply, another customer down the bar got his attention, and he quickly excused himself.

"What did we just do?" Nina asked.

Robin shrugged. "We—or *you*—may just have found TTS's next leading heartthrob. Wouldn't it be a kick if he could really act? He'd be the cutest window dressing we've had in a long time, at any rate."

"I've never done anything like that before. I guess it was just the effect he had on me."

"You and everyone else who meets him, I bet! I'm surprised the bar isn't crowded with slavering females."

"I'm sorry about the remark I made," Nina said after a moment's pause.

"What remark?"

"About our being happily attached and . . ."

"Don't be silly," Robin quickly said, cutting her off. "What's Rafe doing tonight?"

"He went to see a play with one of his old acting-school buddies. Maybe it'll give him an impetus to audition more for the stage. It's what he's really always wanted to do anyway. TTS just keeps a roof over his head." Robin toyed with her cocktail napkin and fell into a deep silence that Nina felt she shouldn't interrupt. She decided to scan the crowd again. Where was Angela?

As Nina looked around, she saw what kind of an "inner circle" they'd entered. She recognized many famous faces from the worlds of fashion, entertainment, politics, and business. This was apparently their new watering hole. Those who gathered here were the froth of New York's crème de la crème. She could read their résumés on their faces— the time-worn and the lovelorn, the flamers and the burnouts, the predators and the prey.

The man who had met them at the door stood in the entry now, his eyes on Nina and Robin. Nina again felt uncomfortable. What *was* it about that man? She turned to ask Robin if she knew him, but when Robin turned to get another look, he was gone.

Nina wondered how Dino would like this place. He'd hate it, she decided. Jule's was filled with the type of people he dealt with every day on the "Silk Stocking" squad, the "simple folks" Dino protected and arrested—and Nina was one of them. That was

one of the major stumbling blocks of their relationship. Dino had old-world Italian ethics and beer-
and-pretzel taste; he couldn't afford to keep up with
a crowd like this and he wouldn't want to. Nina
could, but Dino's macho pride wouldn't let him allow
a woman to pay his way.

Nina sighed and turned around on her stool. Jay
was at the far end of the bar, talking to a customer
who looked as if he'd had a few too many. By the way
Jay was gesturing, it looked as if he was trying to cut
the man off. He was a little taller than Jay, maybe
somewhere in his fifties, but well preserved, perhaps
by the amount of alcohol he drank. He polished off
the drink in his hand, slammed down the glass on the
bar, and disappeared down the back stairway. Jay
wiped off the bar and came back to Nina and Robin,
asking if they'd like a refill. They would.

"Have some trouble down there?" Nina asked
casually.

Jay reacted as though he'd been caught with his
hand in the cookie jar, but he regained his composure
very quickly. "No," he said simply. Nina didn't press.
"I don't think I'm your man," he commented casually
after setting down their fresh drinks.

"What do you mean?" Nina asked.

"Show business. I'm not cut out for it. Present
company excluded, I wouldn't mix too well with
them." Before Nina could reply, he motioned to
another bartender who was passing by, asked him to
take over for a while, and with a polite nod, moved
off and went down the back staircase.

"That was odd," Nina said to herself aloud.

"Brace yourself, Nina," Robin whispered suddenly. "Angela's here, and she's causing quite a stir!"

Nina looked over her shoulder and did a double
take. Nina had chosen her own outfit very carefully
tonight—rust-colored silk, long sleeves—not too
dressy, not too casual. Robin had also chosen some-

41

thing stylish but sedate. Angela, however, was bucking for the big screen.

She stood just a few steps inside the drapes, surveying the crowd with sublime indifference, in her high-collared dark ranch mink cape. Under it, Nina recognized a Jacqueline de Ribes creation in basic black that fit like a second skin. Diamonds glittered in her ears and on her fingers. Her hair was tucked into a black sequined cap, her feet encased in black peau de soie pumps that had rhinestones marching up their backs and continuing on the thin straps that encircled her ankles. Even in this crowd she drew attention—which was, after all, obviously what she'd intended. After just the right amount of time, she finally chose to see Nina and Robin. She waved gaily and sailed across to where they sat. The crowd parted more quickly than the Red Sea had for Moses.

"Darlings," Angela said huskily, "you're *here*! I'm so glad. I hope you didn't have any trouble getting in?"

"Actually . . . ," Nina began.

"Isn't this place just *fabulous*?" Angela said, not allowing Nina to finish.

"Yes," said Robin. "It's incredible."

"I'm so glad you like it. Good—you've got drinks. Let's find a cozy little grotto, kick back, and talk."

"Aren't you going to check your cape?" Nina asked.

"No. Even in a place like this, one never knows what could happen to expensive finery once it's checked and rubbing elbows with clever imitations. Do you *know* how many deceitful things I had to do to get this fur?"

"Why don't you tell us?" Nina said pointedly, with a trace of a smile.

Angela gave her a look. "I mean on the *show*, darling. Several weeks of well-rehearsed bitchery and sweat went into this cape. It goes wherever I go.

42

Traffic was *endless*, and I'm *dying* for a drink. Where's that attractive young bartender with eyes like the Sea of Nepal?"

Robin started laughing. Nina just rolled her eyes. It was going to be quite a night.

After Angela had gotten a rather large manhattan from the relief bartender, the three of them settled onto a camelback sofa and a wing chair that afforded them a view of the room. Angela, still snug as a tick in her cape, finally announced the purpose of the evening.

"I know you haven't the foggiest idea why I invited you here tonight. Now I know this is going to seem very gauche of me, but since there's no one else to do it, I would like to propose a toast. To my birthday! And before anyone gets uncomfortable or timid about asking, I'm fifty-three years old." And with that, she laughed and took a long swallow from her glass.

Nina couldn't believe her ears. Angela Dolan, who guarded her date of birth like Cerberus, had just announced it to the world!

"Drink up or close your mouths," Angela said to Nina and Robin. "I realize my behavior is—well, odd, but I've come to some very important conclusions about life in general. I don't feel, or look, fifty-three if I do say so myself. I'm as young at heart and spirit as either of you. I'm in my prime, and I mean to spend my time with people who *live*, not exist. Nina, you have had more adventures in the past few months than I've had in *years*. Robin, you're young, attractive, and carefree, and I'm going to start being the same. That's why I bought that town house. That's why I wanted the two of you here. And that's why I'm going to drink until the sun rises, *The Turning Seasons* be damned!"

By this point in her monologue, Angela had attracted a sizable amount of attention, including Jay's.

Now at Nina's side, he greeted Angela with a familiar nod, then looked at the other two women.

"Now I know why *The Turning Seasons* sounded familiar. Ms. Dolan, can I get you and your friends anything?"

Nina watched Angela look Jay up and down. Her mind started spinning. Surely *Jay* couldn't be the new man in Angela's life? Though Angela hadn't brought up the subject at all, Nina was sure Horst had been replaced by someone else. But after the terrible experience Helen had had with Rob Bryant, Angela must have more sense than to engage in a May–December romance.

"Good evening, Angie," a second male voice said. Nina turned to see two men standing on Angela's left. One, Nina was surprised to note, was the man she had seen talking to Jay at the end of the bar before they both disappeared down the back stairs. He seemed in control of himself now, and on closer inspection was far more attractive than Nina had first thought. He *was* in his fifties but carried himself like a much younger man. His hair was a radiant silver, but his mustache was still almost coal black.

Angela rose and embraced the man who had just spoken.

"Happy birthday, Angie," he said warmly.

"Thank you. I want you to meet my friends. Nina McFall, Robin Tally, this is Evan Greer, the manager of Jule's."

Robin said hello from across the table. Nina, who was closer, did the same but extended her hand. Evan surprised her by taking it and planting a cool kiss on her warm skin. He was tall and aristocratic looking, with salt-and-pepper hair, high cheekbones, and piercing blue eyes.

Evan turned to the man beside him. "Angie, I want you to meet Dominic Startoni, the owner of

Jule's. He's just returned from out of town . . . unexpectedly."

"Very pleased to meet you," Dominic said with a slight Italian accent. He shook Angela's hand, then bowed in the direction of Nina and Robin. Nina noticed that his accent didn't sound European, but rather Italian-American—rough. Yet his smile was warm and genuine. His hair, dark brown and slightly graying at the temples, would probably have been naturally curly if left to its own devices, but it had obviously been carefully coiffed and straightened professionally. Dark brows arched over heavy-lidded eyes—"bedroom eyes," some might call them, but Nina thought they were the eyes of a dreamer, gentle and a little sad. She liked him instantly, much more so than Evan for some reason.

"Jay," Evan said, "please bring a bottle of Cristal and some glasses. This is Angie's special night." Jay nodded and began to gather up the other glasses and napkins on the table. Evan turned back to Angela. "It's warm in here, sweetheart. Let me take your cape."

"Of course, darling," Angela cooed. Nina and Robin exchanged glances, then Nina audibly gasped as Evan helped Angela remove her cape. There, pinned prominently on the left side of Angela's dress, was the brooch. All heads turned to Nina.

"Are you all right, Ms. McFall?" Evan asked politely.

"Yes," Nina answered, trying to hide her flush of embarrassment. She looked directly at Angela. "I was just . . ."

"Just what, darling?" Angela asked, warning heavy in her voice.

"Nothing," Nina snapped. "I'm sorry. Excuse me for a moment." Nina got up and moved to the bar. In a moment, Angela joined her. "What do you think you're doing with that?" Nina demanded.

45

"*Wearing* it, Nina dear. Now don't be upset. I know it's *your* prop, but as I said this afternoon in the dressing room, it's *just* what the dress needed. A simple touch of PGR. Dennis was sweet enough to let me borrow it for the evening. It will be safe on his desk first thing in the morning. Really, Nina, it's not like it's the crown jewels. Dennis told me he picked it up for twenty dollars or something."

"That's not the point, Angela," Nina said patiently. "They've been looking for just the right piece of jewelry for a long time, and Dennis and Jason would be very upset if anything happened to it."

"Nothing *will*! Now relax and help me enjoy my birthday. What do you think of Evan?" Angela said, almost challengingly.

"I've hardly spent five minutes with him. Are you and he . . . ?"

"Yes! And I've never been happier. He's charming, he's full of life. And he's practically my own age. I feel very lucky, Nina, as lucky as you are with your policeman. Forget this silly brooch thing and say you're happy for me. Please?"

"All right," Nina said. "I'm happy for you, if it's really what you want."

"It is. I vowed never to get too involved with anyone—career and all that. But Evan understands. He's very flexible, not possessive or demanding. We're casual, but committed."

"What about Horst?"

Angela's face clouded for a second. "Horst is a dear, but the chemistry just didn't last. I was too *comfortable* with him. It was like we were an old married couple, and that's *not* what I want, not what I need. I've only known Evan for eight weeks, but I feel as if I've known him much longer. And the excitement never dies. He makes me feel young again." She simpered. "No one's called me 'Angie' since I was a little girl."

"But you're not."

"None of us are, Nina! But flattering allusions to the fact that a part of us still *could* be are very enjoyable. Now just come back to the table. Get to know Evan. That's another reason I wanted you to come tonight."

Angela led Nina back to their seats. Jay and Dominic were gone—Nina assumed that Jay had gone to get the champagne and Dominic to attend to some business. Evan, however, was still there, talking animatedly to Robin. It was clear the young woman was charmed by him. Nina couldn't help wondering how often that happened, and how Evan dealt with it when it did.

Once Nina and Angela had sat down, Robin excused herself to powder her nose and left, with a surreptitious wink at Nina.

"So, did you get my roses?" Evan asked, taking Angela's hand in his.

"Yes, thank you. I took them home and gave them a place of honor in the parlor. The card was beautiful. I tucked it in among the leaves so I can see it every time I walk by."

Evan turned to Nina. "Have you seen Angie's new place yet?"

"No, I haven't. I'm waiting for the big housewarming."

"It's just around the corner," Angela said. "I'm going to throw a *huge* party, one that will make Helen Meyer green with envy. My place may not be as grand as Leatherwing or your fabulous penthouse, Nina dear, but then I don't intend to have *my* party end in disaster as yours and Helen's invariably seem to do."

No argument there, Nina thought wryly.

"Angela says you're something of an amateur sleuth, Nina," Evan commented. Nina shot a blazing glance at Angela.

"What kind of tales has Angela been telling?" she said sweetly, through clenched teeth.

"I have no secrets from Evan," Angela said, fluttering her lashes in Evan's direction. "He has a way of forcing them out. But don't worry—nothing I've said has been indiscreet. Evan *does* read the papers, and when he first learned I was on TTS, he brought up the subject of all the terrible . . . *events* that have been plaguing the show. I merely told him that you're a very sharp judge of character, that you like a good, challenging puzzle, and that you do . . . *stumble* across occasional clues that have been of some help to the NYPD. *Nothing* more."

Nina relaxed a bit.

"Then there *is* more?" Evan asked with a cunning smile.

Nina was saved from answering by Jay, who returned in a rather subdued state with the champagne and glasses. She noted that Evan was looking at him very closely.

"You have a phone call, Mr. Greer," Jay said.

"I'm occupied, Jay. Take a message, please."

"I've already done that, but the party has called several times. I left the messages behind the bar. They're insisting they have to talk to you now, or they'll come right over."

Evan rose with forced casualness, adjusting the jacket of his slate-blue Armani suit. "Where's Dominic?" he asked.

"Upstairs, I believe," Jay replied.

"Since we have to wait for Robin to return before we can have a proper toast anyway," Evan said to them, "I'll just bow out a moment and take care of this. I'll be right back." Evan left the table, Jay gazing after him. After setting up the crystal flutes and arranging the champagne in its silver bucket, he gave Nina and Angela a perfunctory smile and moved away.

"So, Nina, *now* what do you think of Evan?" Angela whispered eagerly.

"He's charming, but . . ."

"But what?"

"I haven't spent that much time with him."

"I thought you had a sixth sense about people," Angela said with a pout.

"I do, sometimes. It's not something I really think about. But I do wish you weren't so free with backstage stories!"

"I told you I hadn't said anything indiscreet. Evan knows nothing about your personal involvement with Detective Rossi. God, I don't have *that* big a mouth! Where on earth is Robin?"

Glad that Angela had changed the subject, Nina swiveled around to check the crowd, and her eyes widened. She hoped against hope that Angela didn't see what she was seeing. Near the back stairwell, their heads just visible, were Robin and Tom Bell.

But Angela had seen. "Well, well, well," she said as she left her seat to join Nina on the couch. "I wonder what *he's* doing here? Do you think Robin will ask him to join us?"

"I'm sure she will," Nina said calmly. "It's not all that surprising that Tom is here."

"No, it's not—particularly since Rafe isn't."

Nina shot her a look as she saw Robin heading their way alone, and the two women did their best to act casual. Robin appeared with a smile but didn't mention Tom, who wasn't with her. Angela broached the subject.

"Was that Tom Bell over there with you, lurking in the shadows?" she asked innocently.

"Yes," Robin replied. "Strange coincidence that he should be here, too."

"*Very*," Angela said.

"Why didn't you ask him to join us?" Nina asked.

"I did, but he was on his way out. He sends his regards."

"You didn't tell him about my birthday, did you, dear?" Angela asked anxiously.

"No. We really didn't talk that long."

Angela raised an eyebrow and looked at Nina, who said nothing. Suddenly they heard a commotion outside—loud, angry male voices. An instant later, all three women gasped as the red drapes parted violently and Horst Krueger burst into the room. He collided with several people, mumbled a quick apology and waded further into the crowd. It was immediately clear to Nina that he'd been drinking. As Horst saw Angela and started to stride toward her, the bearded man and the money taker from downstairs also appeared. Angela rose just as Horst arrived at their table.

"What on earth are you doing here? How did you get in?" she hissed.

"Where is he?" Horst demanded, his speech a little slurred.

Nina tried to step in before there was serious trouble. "Horst, please! This isn't the time or place for this!"

Horst ignored her, glaring at Angela. The crowd was edging away from them, the bouncers advancing. Nina looked around frantically, hoping that Jay might be able to help them, but he was nowhere in sight.

"I want you to leave this instant," Angela commanded, "before you make a spectacle of yourself and embarrass us all!"

"I think you've done a pretty good job on your own," Horst shot back. "I just want to know what he looks like so I can put my fist through his face the next time I see him."

"Wild talk like that isn't going to solve anything, Horst," Nina pleaded.

"You're right, Nina. *Talk* isn't going to solve anything at all. I'm ready for action!"

As the two burly guardians of Jule's came forward to remove Horst from the premises, his strength and agility caught them both off guard. He elbowed Moneybags in the midsection, then swung around and caught the bearded man with a right hook. Both staggered, but neither went down. The fascinated crowd buzzed and murmured, eager to see what would happen next.

"What's going on here?" a voice demanded. Nina turned in dismay and saw Evan advancing. The expression on Angela's face gave her away—Horst knew he was facing his rival. Without a word, he sprang forward with incredible speed and would have attacked Evan if the two rounders hadn't grappled him to the floor.

"I'll get you, you miserable son of a bitch!" Horst yelled as he was dragged out. "I swear it!"

Evan consoled Angela with comforting arms as Nina tried to decide whether to go after Horst. She started to stand up, but Robin grabbed her arm and shook her head.

For once, just leave things alone, Nina said to herself. After all, no real harm was done. Nobody was hurt. Things could have been a lot worse.

"I'm sorry that had to happen, Angie," Evan said earnestly. "I'll make it a point to find out how he got in. It won't happen again, I promise."

"I think Horst was just letting a few drinks do his talking for him. He's not usually like this. He's just . . . hurt," Nina said with a dark look at Angela. But Angela avoided Nina's gaze.

"Let's put this all behind us and have that champagne, all right?" Evan suggested. Angela nodded, stifling tears of embarrassment and what looked to Nina like genuine guilt. Evan popped the cork with aplomb, poured the drinks, then lifted his glass. "To

51

Angie, my angel. Happy birthday to the prettiest girl that heaven has ever sent me!" Now Angela let the tears flow. Evan seemed distant for a moment, as if totally preoccupied with something other than Angela. Then he put an arm around her shoulders and held her close. Robin and Nina offered their own congratulations, and shortly thereafter everything returned to normal.

Two bottles of champagne later, Evan asked Angela to dance, leaving Nina and Robin to their own devices. Nina tried to bring up the subject of Tom Bell, but Robin quickly changed the subject and excused herself to phone Rafe.

Alone, and seeing Jay once again behind the bar, Nina felt like talking. She was halfway there when a sultry, well-endowed blonde deliberately cut in front of her and took the only empty stool. It happened to be directly in front of Jay, who smiled warmly, if a bit mechanically, and automatically gave her a drink. A regular, Nina assumed, since Jay seemed to know exactly what she wanted. By the way the blonde was leaning over the bar, she did, too.

Nina wandered back toward her seat, only to find it taken. She was feeling a little unsteady—the mixture of champagne and gimlets was going straight to her head. You should have eaten more—or drunk less, she scolded herself. Then she noticed Angela's cape within easy reach over the back of the sofa where Evan had left it. Good thinking on everyone's part to just leave it there, she thought. Setting her glass down and rescuing the fur, Nina decided to get some air. She glided across the room, parted the curtains, and moved into the second-floor foyer.

It was deserted. She walked to the railing and peered down at the winding stairs. Nina repressed a feeling of vertigo and hastily stepped back. Her eye happened to fall on the "forbidden staircase" to the third floor and, after checking around, she casually sauntered toward it.

"That's off limits," a woman's voice suddenly said behind her. Startled, Nina whirled around and dropped Angela's cape. The speaker was the same blonde who'd plopped herself down in front of Nina at the bar. She was leaning against the archway like a forties glamour girl. Her hair, tortured by some new-wave beautician, framed her face like an electric mane. Ruby nails toyed with a long strand of pearls tied in a loose knot that lay against her full breasts. She was wearing a dark blue stretch tulle bodysuit, red sequined pants, and navy pumps. Nina knew the outfit was expensive, but somehow it looked cheap on this woman. Nina picked up Angela's fur.

"I was just looking around," she said lamely.

"Mr. Startoni wouldn't like it," the woman replied. "Especially while he's away." Nina was about to inform her that Dominic had returned, but decided against it.

"Are you a friend of Mr. Startoni's?" she asked.

"An acquaintance. I know everybody here. Nice stuff," the woman added, running her blood-red nails over Angela's cape. "Must have cost a wad."

"It's not mine. I'm just holding it for a friend," Nina said. She was anxious to get away from this woman, who was making her strangely uncomfortable. She was smiling at Nina now, her expression almost feral. "And speaking of my friend," Nina continued, "I think I should collect her. It's getting late."

"Late?" the woman exclaimed with a laugh. "The night's just revving up!"

At that moment, Angela and Evan moved onto the balcony. The woman saw them first and reacted sharply. Both women saw Angela slip something into the palm of Evan's hand with a smile. He pulled her into his arms, the two of them oblivious to Nina and

53

the blonde. Nina was about to excuse herself and join them, but the blonde was already halfway across the floor, a certain stiffness in her gait.

Nina greeted Angela and Evan and suggested that she and Angela leave. To Nina's surprise, Angela agreed. As Evan took the cape and was tenderly draping it over her shoulders, Nina caught a glimpse of the blonde peering through the drapes on the far side of the balcony. Then with a vicious flick of her wrists, she closed them tightly and was gone.

"Where's Robin?" Angela asked.

"She went to call Rafe a few minutes ago . . . and here she is now," Nina said as Robin came over to the group.

"Thought you'd all left without me," she commented.

"I was just about to look for you," Nina said.

Evan bid Nina and Robin a gracious good night, then smiled lovingly at Angela, wished her a happy birthday again, and told her to sleep well. Angela smirked and gave him a wink. He returned it, then disappeared into the game room.

"It's just been a *dream* of an evening!" Angela said with a contented sigh. "And I can't thank the two of you enough for coming. I sincerely appreciate it."

They started down the staircase and had just reached the first floor when Angela stopped.

"Nina, did any of us leave Jay a tip?" she asked.

"I didn't," said Robin. "I would have if I'd known we were leaving."

"I didn't, either," Nina admitted.

"He's such a charming, personable boy. A bit too serious at times, but a dear. I want to leave him something for his efforts."

Nina dug out her coat-check stub and gave it to Robin. "Will you get our coats? I'll just run back up with Angela and say good night for both of us." Robin agreed and started across the foyer as Nina and

Angela went back up the stairs and entered the main barroom.

Nina saw them first.

They were in the shadows, but it was unmistakably Evan and the blonde. He was cupping her face in his hands, while she had her arms around his waist under his jacket, her body pressed closely against his. Before she could divert Angela's attention, Nina felt her stiffen beside her. Glancing apprehensively at Angela, she saw steel in her eyes as she silently watched Evan and the woman. Without another word, Angela turned sharply on her heel, thrust the drapes apart and left.

Nina glanced back at Evan. He hadn't seen them. Trying to catch up with Angela and fumbling through the drapes, she bumped into the bearded bouncer, who offered her a crooked grin. She excused herself and hurried out onto the balcony. She could hear the staccato taps of Angela's heels echoing down the staircase. By the time Nina reached the vestibule, Angela was just brushing past Robin and heading outside.

"What's wrong?" Robin asked when Nina joined her. "Angela looks upset."

"That could very well be the understatement of the year! I'll explain later, honey," Nina murmured, taking her coat and heading for the door. "Angela's happy birthday just took a nosedive."

About half an hour later, after getting a cab and dropping a very puzzled Robin off at her apartment, Nina was sitting with a stone-faced Angela in a little booth in an East Side cocktail lounge. Angela hadn't spoken five words since they'd left Jule's, and Nina was trying desperately to think of something to say.

Angela was swilling manhattans. Nina looked into the bottom of her glass of Perrier, wondering if she should simply have gone home. No, she said to herself, you did the right thing. Angela is more vulnerable than you've ever seen her. She needs *somebody*—how odd that somebody is you. She saw Angela check her watch, then signal the waitress.

"Angela," Nina began hesitantly, "don't you think you've . . ."

"Nina, please!" Angela cut her off, her voice quiet but firm. "I appreciate your being here, but *no* advice, *no* lectures, *no* trite words of comfort. I've been living in a fool's paradise. I realize that, and I'll deal with it in my own way . . . soon." She checked her watch for the third or fourth time as the waitress brought her yet another drink. Nina had no idea what she meant by that remark but sincerely hoped that Angela didn't plan on going back to Jule's and confronting Evan while she was in this frame of mind.

"It's late, Angela. We both have to work tomorrow," Nina pointed out.

"I can't go home. Not yet," Nina replied flatly. There was a long pause, then she looked up at Nina. "You didn't like him, did you?"

"I didn't have much opportunity to form an opinion one way or the other," Nina offered diplomatically.

"I've had *plenty* of opportunity," Angela muttered. "I guess *my* opinion was dead wrong!" For a moment, she looked on the verge of tears, but some inner core of strength and self-preservation prevented her from giving in to self-pity. Nina admired her for that.

"Let things settle a little, Angela," Nina advised, now that Angela had finally started to talk about it. "Maybe . . ."

"Maybe what?" Angela snapped. "Maybe there was a logical explanation for what we saw? That she's his daughter perhaps, or a wayward niece? No, Nina, there is *no* explanation except the obvious one." And with that, she downed her drink, checked her dia-

56

mond watch again, and sank into impenetrable silence once more.

The brooch caught Nina's attention. It seemed to capture the dim light in the lounge and feed on it, doubling its brilliance. Again, Nina thought about drops of blood and shuddered.

Nina insisted on seeing Angela home once she was finally ready to leave. It was now after one in the morning. Angela nearly fell out of the cab when it pulled up in front of her East Sixty-third Street address. Nina paid the driver and sent him on his way before Angela could collect herself enough to protest.

"I'll come in and make some coffee," Nina suggested.

"No!" Angela said immediately. Nina stared at her, and Angela quickly shifted gears. "Just see me up the steps—I'll be fine." Nina didn't know if it was the cold wind or sheer determination that had sobered Angela up, but the clarity was back in her eyes and her voice. She nimbly mounted the steps, then paused to fish her keys out of her purse. "Thank you, Nina. I'm sorry *both* of us had to be exposed to that tacky little scene tonight. I would appreciate it if it were all forgotten by tomorrow."

Nina realized that wasn't a simple request—it was a demand. "Are you sure you don't want me to come in?" she persisted.

"Yes," Angela said firmly. She slipped a key into the lock, opened the door, and disappeared inside. Nina pulled her collar up against the wind and started down the steps. She paused for a moment before heading over to Madison Avenue to hail another cab, looking up at Angela's new home. She saw a light go on inside and cast a soft glow into the night. Despite their differences, Nina felt genuinely sorry for Angela. Regardless of what kind of man Evan Greer really was, he had made her blissfully happy for at least a brief time. God only knew what Angela would do now that the bubble had burst.

Nina was more than halfway down the block when she suddenly decided that whether Angela wanted her there or not, she simply couldn't leave the poor woman alone to nurse her misery and rage. She turned and began to retrace her steps, determined to offer what comfort she could. It was as she started to mount the stairs to Angela's house that she heard the scream from inside.

Nina took the remaining few steps two at a time and tried the door. It was locked, of course. She began ringing the doorbell furiously, but Angela didn't answer. Then she pounded on the door, loudly calling Angela's name, not caring who heard her. Apparently no one did. Seemingly endless minutes passed as Nina tried to decide what to do next. Then the front door slowly opened a crack, and Angela's stricken face appeared, devoid of color. It seemed to Nina that Angela was staring *through* her, not *at* her.

"Angela, I heard a scream. What is it? What's wrong?"

Angela backed out of sight and opened the door a little farther. Nina nervously sidled past her. "Angela, please, what is it? Tell me!"

Angela silently pointed down a long entrance hall, past an imposing staircase that dominated the foyer. Light streamed from an open door. Nina hurried toward the room as Angela closed and locked the front door. Bracing herself, she dashed through the doorway.

Her first glimpse of the room brought into focus a black grand piano, a fringed white shawl draped across the closed lid. A bouquet of dark red roses in a cut-crystal vase was centrally and dramatically placed on top of it.

58

Then she saw the body.

The supine figure of a man lay on the plush mauve carpet.

As Nina crept closer, she realized that it was Evan Greer. His nose was grotesquely disfigured, pushed in. There was dark discoloration under his eyes. Fighting fear and revulsion, Nina put herself on automatic pilot and knelt to feel his pulse.

"Don't bother," Angela said tonelessly as she drifted into the room. "He's dead."

Chapter Four

Angela leaned against the doorframe and closed her eyes. For the moment, she seemed to be holding up all right, so Nina examined the body—she'd been through this before, but she knew she'd *never* get used to it.

There was no sign that Evan was breathing. She searched for a pulse on Evan's neck the way Dino had told her to do; it was one of the easiest and most reliable places to look. His skin was warm to the touch, but there was no telltale throbbing to indicate that his heart was still pumping blood through his veins.

"*He's dead!*" Angela suddenly shrieked, losing all control. "I told you he's dead. Just stop it and get away from him, for God's sake!" Her body went slack and she stumbled over to the piano and gripped it for support. Then she slowly sank down onto the bench and began to sob.

Nina went to her and rested her palms on Angela's heaving shoulders. She remembered Angela's last words about wanting what they'd witnessed at Jule's "all forgotten by tomorrow." It wouldn't be, not now. This would be just the beginning. After a moment, Angela slid out from under Nina's touch, got up with regained composure, and stared down at Evan's corpse.

"You knew he was coming, didn't you, Angela?" Nina said quietly. "That's why you kept checking your watch."

"Don't you have a call to make, Nina?" Angela said, ignoring the question. "The sooner Detective Rossi gets here . . ." Her voice trailed off with a slight quiver.

Nina nodded. "You're right. Dino isn't on duty, but I'll call him at home right away."

"There's a phone in the kitchen. I think I could also use that coffee you wanted to make."

"Of course, Angela. Let's *both* go into the kitchen and . . ."

"No. I want to stay here for a minute."

"I don't think that's wise." Nina tried to steer Angela out, but she remained firmly rooted to the spot.

"I won't touch anything, if that's what you're worried about. I know the procedure well enough by now."

"It's *you* I'm worried about," Nina said softly.

Angela looked into her eyes for a few seconds, then back at Evan, and finally tottered over to the marble fireplace that graced the other end of the parlor. She scanned the room and, in a voice thick with conflicting emotions, said, "It's going to take one helluva housewarming to take the chill off this place now, isn't it?"

"Angela . . ."

"Make the call, Nina. Time is too precious to waste. I learn that more and more every day."

Nina decided to leave Angela alone long enough to call Dino. She made her way back into the hall, found the kitchen, and turned on the lights. She punched Dino's number with a weary finger and listened to several rings before Dino's deep voice, made huskier by sleep, answered the phone.

"Dino, it's Nina."

"What's wrong?" he asked, suddenly alert. Nina felt a tingle of warmth and reassurance just hearing him.

"I'm with Angela. I'm afraid it's happened again. Could you come over?"

Nina gave a brief explanation and told him the address. Dino said he'd be there as soon as possible. Then Nina hung up and looked for the coffee things. While she was filling the pot with water, Angela passed by the kitchen door but didn't respond when Nina called her name.

Trying to get her churning thoughts in order, Nina concentrated hard. The fact that Evan's body was still warm led her to realize that he hadn't been dead very long—maybe half an hour. Maybe minutes . . .

Nina suddenly had a truly hair-raising thought. Ignoring the nagging possibility that *Angela* had killed Evan, she realized that if he had been murdered moments before Angela came home, the killer could still be in the house!

She whirled at a sound behind her in the shadowy breakfast nook, only to see one of Angela's three cats creep out of a corner and stare at her with moon-bright eyes. She didn't know which one it was—Marietta, Mame, or Molly Brown. All were named in homage to Broadway musicals, the professional medium Angela had once dreamed of conquering, a goal she had never accomplished. The cat was cautiously sniffing Nina's discarded coat and purse, which she had thrown over the countertop before preparing the coffee.

Relieved but still fearful, Nina ran out of the kitchen, calling Angela. She found her in the living room, standing nervously behind a library table that boasted an elaborate bar setup. She held a rocks glass in one shaking had, and her eyes were as wide and luminous as the cat's had been. "I—I couldn't wait for the coffee," she said, suddenly fumbling with a crystal stopper on a decanter. "I . . . I need a brandy." Her voice was high-pitched and tense.

"I just had a very disturbing thought," Nina whispered, coming over to her. "Did you hear any noises when you first came home, or any since you've been here?"

"No—why?"

"What if the killer is still here and heard us outside, heard you come in. . . . "

"There's no one else here but us," Angela snapped, shakily pouring the amber liquor into the glass. She was gripping the tumbler so hard with her other hand that her knuckles were turning white. The other two cats appeared, a snowy Angora and a buff-colored Persian. Angela lurched from behind the bar to greet her pets, but didn't set her glass down. Even under the circumstances, Nina felt she was acting very strangely.

"My babies wouldn't be roaming about if there was someone strange in the house. That's how I . . . I knew something was wrong the moment I walked in. They didn't come running into the hall to meet me. Now they're fine." The cat from the breakfast nook, a chocolate-toned Himalayan, crept softly into the room. "There's my Molly Brown!" Anglea cooed. "Thank God no one hurt any of my babies!" She stroked and petted each cat in turn, always careful to hold on to her brandy, though as yet she hadn't even taken the smallest sip. "Don't you think we should—cover Evan with something until your detective arrives? I have blankets and afghans upstairs in the hall closet."

Was Angela trying to get Nina out of the room? "I

don't think we should disturb anything until Dino and his men have a chance to go over the place. I was very careful to handle things as little as possible in the kitchen. I hope you did the same in here."

"Of course I did! I mean, I didn't touch anything except when I poured myself this drink. I hardly think the killer had refreshments on his mind after he did away with Evan!"

"He—or she," Nina replied.

Angela looked her squarely in the eye. "You think I may have done it, do you? No, don't answer that, please." Now she gulped down the brandy, clutching the glass with both hands, and headed back for more.

The doorbell rang.

"I'll get it," Nina said. "Try to relax."

"So I'll look less suspicious?" Angela asked dryly.

Nina refrained from saying anything and went to answer the door. She heard Angela go into the kitchen and start running water. What was she doing? Nina finally opened the door to find Dino, Sergeant Charley Harper, and two members of the crime squad on the doorstep. "Thanks for coming so soon, Lieutenant," Nina said formally as the group moved in.

"Don't mention it, Ms. McFall," Dino responded equally formally, his eyes already taking in the layout of the town house. "Where's the body?"

"Right down the hall. Ms. Dolan is in the kitchen." Their stilted exchange was a previously-agreed-upon arrangement she and Dino always used in public. When Nina had first opened the door and seen his dark curly hair and sleep-haunted gray eyes, she'd had to restrain herself from throwing her arms around his massive chest and resting her head on his shoulder. But she kept her emotions firmly in check.

"Lead the way, Ms. McFall," Dino said.

As they reached the kitchen, Angela stepped into

the hall, wiping her hands, like Lady Macbeth, on a linen dish towel. Angela and Dino exchanged strained greetings and then Angela led the way into the parlor. Nina saw Dino wince when he saw Evan Greer's mutilated face.

"He's dead, Lieutenant," Nina said. "I checked for a pulse—there wasn't any, but his skin was still warm to the touch."

"Good," said Dino crisply. "Charley, you and the boys know what to do. Go over everything and see what you come up with."

As Dino's men sprang into action, he turned to Angela, who was staring fixedly at her bouquet of roses. "Ms. Dolan, could I please talk to you in another room?" Angela said nothing. "Ms. Dolan?" Dino repeated.

"What?" she said, her trance broken.

"I'd like to ask you some questions. Privately."

Angela looked beseechingly at Nina.

"Would you mind if I sat in, Lieutenant Rossi?" Nina asked.

"Not at all."

"Angela, let's all go into the kitchen. We can sit in the breakfast nook," Nina suggested.

Angela cast a disapproving glance at Dino's men. "I have some very valuable things in this house. Is it necessary that they sully every objet d'art that I own? And I have pets. Purebred cats. Their delicate systems have already been traumatized once this evening." The policemen looked nonplused.

"It's purely routine, Ms. Dolan," Dino said smoothly. "And my boys are very careful. Go to it, guys . . . and watch the expensive stuff, okay?" They nodded, and Dino indicated that Angela should go first. She left the room, her state of agitation obviously growing. Dino and Nina followed her into the kitchen, and Nina caught a glimpse of two of Angela's cats dashing for cover.

"I made coffee. Would you like some, Lieutenant?" Nina asked.

"No, but maybe Ms. Dolan would," Dino replied.

Angela glared at him. "I *have* been drinking. Quite a bit, as a matter of fact, but my mind is perfectly clear, thank you!"

As Dino and Angela took opposite seats in the nook, Nina wandered casually over to the sink. She scanned the area. Had Angela washed out her glass? If so, where was it?

"Ms. McFall told me on the phone that you discovered the body, Ms. Dolan."

"Yes, I did."

"And you know this man?"

"Yes. His name is Evan Greer."

"How long have the two of you been acquainted?"

"About two months. We were—involved. It's no secret. Nina and I had both been with him earlier tonight at Jule's, the club he manages. That's where Evan and I first met."

"What time was that?"

"What time did we first meet, when did Nina and I last see him, or what time did I find the body?" Angela asked with a trace of irritation.

"The last two," Dino replied patiently.

"I'm not sure what time we left the club, but Nina and I arrived here a little after one."

"I think," Nina spoke up, "we left the club about eleven-thirty."

"Do you know," Dino continued, "how Mr. Greer gained access into your home?"

Angela hesitated, then looked at Nina before she spoke. "I gave him a key this evening."

That must have been what Angela had given Evan on the balcony, Nina thought.

"What time did you expect him?" Dino asked.

"Around one. He often took a break at that time.

Jule's is officially open until four, but Evan's hours are—were—flexible."

"Did anyone else know he was coming here tonight?"

"Not that I know of," Angela said.

"But he has been here before at that time?"

"Yes, but usually on weekends, or sometimes when I'd been written out of the script for the next day. That means . . ."

"I know what it means," Dino said. "It means you got the day off. Now think, Ms. Dolan. Do you know anyone who might have wanted to harm Mr. Greer, or why?"

Angela and Nina glanced at each other, and Angela said promptly, "No. But I suppose a man in his profession might make enemies."

"Tell me exactly what happened when you came in this evening."

"Nina saw me home. I left her on the steps, and . . ."

"Excuse me," Dino interrupted. "It's after one. Ms. McFall sees you home, and you leave her on the steps? Was the cab waiting?"

"No," Angela said. "I hadn't realized the cab had driven away until I noticed Nina beside me. I told her I was fine. I knew Evan would probably be waiting for me, and I wanted to be alone with him."

"I can understand that," Dino said.

"You don't understand anything!" Angela snapped, suddenly rising and moving out from under Dino's steady gaze. "Nina's going to tell you this at some point anyway, so you might as well hear it from me first! It wasn't going to be the evening of high romance I'd originally been looking forward to."

"Why is that?" Dino asked.

"Evan was being unfaithful to me," Angela blurted.

"You don't know that, Angela," Nina said quickly.

"What does it matter now, Nina?" Angela replied,

67

her shoulders sagging in defeat. "I may be vain, but I'm not stupid. The differences between me and *that woman* are all too obvious. I just didn't think Evan was the type to be attracted to that sort."

"Could we back up a mintue?" Dino asked. "*What* woman?"

Angela proceeded to tell Dino about going back to leave the bartender a tip and seeing Evan with the blonde. Her narrative was almost detached, as if she'd been a casual observer of the scene. Dino, however, was not deceived.

"So you were angry?" he asked.

"To say the least!" Angela replied. She absently picked up the dish towel she'd discarded earlier and began wringing it in her hands. "Nina can attest to the fact that I went out to drown my sorrows, as well as to fortify myself for the scene I knew was coming when I finally got home."

"And what did you plan to say to Mr. Greer?"

"Things I'm sure would make some of your most jaded fellow officers blush," Angela replied matter-of-factly. "Then I was going to kick him out of this house and out of my life."

Dino mulled this over, then went on. "When you came in tonight, what happened?"

"The house was quiet. A light was on in the parlor. The rest of the house was dark."

"Did you find that unusual?"

"No—I often leave the parlor light on. I hate coming home to total darkness. What *was* unusual was the fact that my cats didn't come out to welcome me. I turned on the hall light, but there was no sign of them. They knew Evan. They even liked him, in the indifferent sort of way that cats do. I called to them, but they still didn't come. So I walked down the hall, into the parlor—and saw Evan."

"That must have been when I heard you scream," Nina said. "I immediately rang the bell," she told

Dino. "When Angela didn't answer right away, I became very concerned."

"Why didn't you answer the door right away, Ms. Dolan?" Dino asked.

"I was in a state of shock, Lieutenant! I'd just found a *dead man* on my new carpet! I didn't even hear the bell. Then I realized that someone was pounding on the front door, and I opened it to Nina. You know the rest." Dino studied her. "It's written all over your face, Lieutenant," Angela said quietly.

"What is?" Dino asked.

"You think I did it. You think I certainly had a motive as well as opportunity. And my mind was clouded enough by liquor and rage to—ignore the consequences of such an action. A 'crime of passion'—isn't that what you people call it?"

"*Did* you kill him, Ms. Dolan?" Dino asked, his eyes riveted on her. Nina held her breath.

"No, I didn't," Angela finally answered. "But the thought had crossed my mind. Of that, I'm surely guilty!"

Sergeant Harper appeared in the doorway. "We're all done. You want us to check things here?"

"Do that," Dino answered. "You didn't touch any doors or windows when you got home, did you, Ms. Dolan?"

"Only the front door."

"Ms. McFall?"

"No."

"All right. Then if somebody else was in the house, we should try to figure out how they got in—and out. Let's give the boys their shot in here," Dino said to the two women, rising.

Nina gathered up her coat and purse, and she, Angela, and Dino left the kitchen single file as Charley and Paul came in. "I called an ambulance to get the body and notified the medical examiner," Paul told Dino.

"Thanks," Dino said. Nina looked into Dino's eyes, trying to get some clue as to what was going on in his head. His expression, as usual, did not betray his thoughts.

Angela paused in the hall. "Would it be all right if I went upstairs and changed, Lieutenant?" Dino nodded. Angela started up the stairs, then turned and removed the brooch. "Here," she said, thrusting it at Nina. "Take this while I still remember to give it to you. I don't know if I'll be going to the studio tomorrow, and I don't want it lying around here as a reminder of this evening. Thank Dennis for letting me borrow it. And if you're not still here when I come down . . . thank *you*."

Nina embraced Angela, her coat and purse still over her arm. "Would you like me to spend the night?" she offered.

"There's really no need," Angela replied. Looking down at Dino, she said, "This is going to generate a great deal of ugly publicity, isn't it, Lieutenant?"

"Possibly," Dino said. "I'll do what I can to soft-pedal things, but . . ."

"I understand," Angela sighed. "Nina, I suppose someone should inform Helen about all this before she reads the morning headlines and has a stroke."

"I'll call her, Angela," Nina promised.

Angela then slowly mounted the carpeted stairs, calling for her pets.

Dino turned to Nina. "So," he said wearily. "You're in the thick of it again. A lot of possibilities ran through my brain when you told me you had plans tonight, but this wasn't one of them. Guess I should have known better."

Oh, how Nina wanted him to touch her! She wondered if Dino felt the same. She wanted to ask him, wanted to hear his deep voice say something loving and reassuring. For a moment they looked into each other's eyes.

"How . . . how did he die?" Nina asked, losing her nerve.

"Instantly," Dino replied crisply, but Nina thought she saw a trace of longing just below the surface of his professional demeanor. "I've gotta call the station," he added. "Why don't you go in the living room, sit down, and collect your thoughts? I want to hear your reactions, instincts, and observations about everything that happened tonight from the time you met Mr. Greer until now. You know—the stuff you're so damn good at."

"Sometimes I wish I wasn't," Nina said softly.

She watched Dino's broad back as he strode down the hall and entered the kitchen. Then she obediently went into the living room and plunked herself down on an extravagantly floral chintz sofa, realizing she still held the brooch in her hand. She dropped it into her purse, which she was about to place on the marble coffee table when she saw the water rings.

There were two of them. The smaller looked as if it had been made by a glass, the larger by a bottle. Nina closed her eyes, forcing her mind back to when she had passed the open door to this room on her way to the parlor. She couldn't swear to it, but she thought she'd seen something on the table, reflecting the light. Now the table was empty, as it had been when Nina walked in and found Angela about to pour that brandy.

Nina went to the library table and checked the bar supplies. She saw several decanters, a few bottles of liqueur, and a number of glasses on a silver tray—four brandy snifters, four cordial glasses, but only three rocks glasses. Why had Angela taken one of those for her brandy instead of a snifter? And if it had indeed been that same glass she'd been washing in the kitchen, why had she done so? Was she trying to remove some incriminating evidence?

71

Nina simply couldn't believe that Angela was capable of murder, particularly such a brutal one, but it seemed clear that she was hiding something, both from Nina and from the police.

Chapter Five

A cold spring morning was just struggling to fulfill its promise of warmth through the drift of clouds that huddled over the Hudson River at five-forty-five that morning. Nina, her face bathed in the steam from her sixth or seventh cup of Earl Grey tea, stood staring out the windows of her Riverside Drive penthouse. Sleep had been impossible after Dino had brought her home from Angela's.

Nina had been weary and silent when she got into the front seat of Dino's car. But once he'd joined her and let his engine idle as the ambulance bearing Evan Greer's body sped away, she felt the need to talk about something other than murder.

"How was the hockey game?" she asked.

Dino smiled. "Great. Peter had a good time. But he wanted to know why you didn't come with us."

"What did you tell him?"

"The truth—that I never thought to ask you to a hockey game. I didn't think it was your style. He said I was wrong." He reached over and squeezed her hand. "Was I?" Nina's heart melted. She leaned over and kissed him softly on the cheek. His unshaven face grated on her lips.

"Wrong to say it wasn't my style, or wrong not to ask me?"

"Either."

"Next time you get some hot tickets—unless they're for mud wrestling—give me a call and you'll find out." Dino smiled, then looked out the window at Angela's town house and grew serious. Nina knew he was thinking about everything she'd told him about the evening's events. She'd described Jule's in detail, and mentioned meeting Evan, Dominic, and even Jay, who she thought might be helpful. Jay seemed observant—there was no telling what he might know or have seen after Angela and Nina had left.

Then there was the bearded man. While Nina told Dino about him, she suddenly remembered his smile when she followed Angela after witnessing Evan with the blonde. It was almost as if he knew what was going on and was perversely enjoying it. Dino said he'd check the man out. Nina *had*, however, left out one minor detail—the scene with Horst Krueger. Horst wasn't any more capable of murder than Angela, no matter how much he'd had to drink. No sense in sending Dino off on a wild-goose chase.

"*Hapkido*," Dino said quietly.

"*What*?" Nina said, startled.

"*Hapkido*. It's a kind of martial-arts move—a tactic of Korean street fighting. That's what killed Evan Greer. One well-aimed shot with the palm of your hand in the nose and *pow*—the nasal bone is projected right up into the victim's brain. Death is instantaneous."

Nina was horrified. "Have you ever seen it before?" she asked.

"Charley has. He was on a beat down in Chinatown for a while. It's a pretty common move. You can

74

learn it in a self-defense course, in the Marine Corps, even on the street, if your life has been rough enough. I've heard of cases where hookers and hustlers have used it on freaked-out johns."

"Good Lord!" Nina whispered.

"Whoever went after Greer knew exactly what they were doing; no muss, no fuss, no risk of retaliation." He put the car in gear and began to cruise Sixty-third Street to Madison Avenue, then turned uptown. The streets were cold and empty— just the way Nina felt inside. They drove in silence for a while. When they stopped for a red light on Seventy-ninth Street, Dino asked abruptly, "You have any idea what Angela's hiding?"

The question shocked Nina. She hadn't mentioned her discovery of the water rings on Angela's table— she was sure they didn't really mean anything.

"No," she said simply.

"But you *do* agree she's hiding something?" Dino pressed.

"I—I don't know," Nina faltered.

"She cleaned up some things in the living room before we got there—at least, that's the impression the boys got. They found some male prints on the coffee table. There were more of the same prints on a bottle of crème de menthe. You see Greer knock any of that stuff down at this club?"

"No. Nothing but champagne."

"I tried the stuff once—like drinking honey and Chloraseptic. Give me good old dago red any day." Dino flashed her a broad grin. Nina knew he was trying to lighten the mood, and for a moment he had, but she was soon worrying again.

She could imagine Evan sipping the green liqueur in Angela's living room while waiting for her to return. But if he had, why would Angela try to conceal the fact?

"You don't really think that Angela . . ." Nina couldn't finish.

"She never asked how Greer died," Dino pointed out.

"I can't believe she did this," Nina said flatly.

"I can't dismiss the possibility. Let's face it— Angela had a damn good motive. I know the kind of anger that hurt and jealousy can stir up in somebody." Dino gripped the wheel, and Nina knew he was thinking about his betrayal by his ex-wife. She made no response, hoping the memory would die a natural death.

Soon they were parked outside Primrose Towers. Dino insisted on seeing her up to her penthouse, which Nina didn't mind at all. They rode the elevator in silence and when they entered her private foyer, Dino pulled her into his arms.

"I've wanted you to do this all evening," she whispered into his ear.

"Me, too, babe. I'd see you all the way into your apartment, but I might not get out again. You need rest, and I have to follow up on some things. If you think of anything else, give me a call. Otherwise, I'll be in touch." He kissed her fiercely but tenderly, and his strong fingers pressed against the small of her back with passionate urgency. But they both knew that, for the moment, it had to end right there.

Now, as the morning sky suddenly darkened with the advent of more thick clouds, Nina wished Dino had stayed. If only they could act like any ordinary couple in love—but something always seemed to blemish the picture . . .

Nina decided to take a shower, hoping the stinging needles of hot water would revitalize her for the long day ahead. She roughly toweled herself dry, trying to get her blood moving, while Chessy sat on the bath mat, his yellow eyes seeming to take her in with male appreciation. Nina smiled and chucked the brawny tom under the chin. He seemed miffed at this meager demonstration of affection and sauntered out through the crack of the door, tail held high in feline indignation. Nina suddenly thought of Marietta, Mame, and Molly Brown. If they could only talk! *They* knew who else had been in Angela's town house last night.

By the time Nina was dressed and Chessy had polished off a hearty breakfast, it was still too early to go to the studio. It was also raining. What a dismal day this is going to be, Nina thought wearily. Then, remembering her promise to Angela, she looked up the number of the Meyer estate and called Helen. She hoped she was already up. This wouldn't be a pleasant call under the best of circumstances.

"Hello?" Helen sounded wide awake, thank God.

"Helen, it's Nina."

"If you're calling to tell me about Angela, I already know," Helen snapped. "I just got off the phone with her."

Nina was surprised. "How did she sound?"

"Like hell," Helen responded coldly. "I've put in a call to the studio to alert them to the swarm of reporters who'll inevitably be descending when this sweet little piece of news gets out. I don't want *anyone* from the show talking to them except me. *Is that clear?*"

"Yes, Helen."

"I'll make the usual blanket statement. Lord knows it's well rehearsed by now! Angela still doesn't know if she's coming in today or not. I guess I'll have to deal with that when I get to the studio, but the writers have been warned they may have to do some last-minute sleight of hand around Angela's scenes."

"What about Horst?" Nina asked. "Shouldn't he . . ."

"I've tried calling him, but there's no answer. And now I want to get something straight. Leave this one alone, Nina. Let the police handle it. Outside of Angela, it has *nothing* to do with TTS or anyone else connected to it, *you* included. I'll see you at the studio."

Nina reacted to the sudden dial tone. Today was going to be even more dismal than she'd thought.

As bad luck would have it, Nina was late getting to the studio. She had wanted to touch base with Angela, but Angela wasn't answering her phone. Then she tried Dino, only to learn that he was out. Nina refrained from leaving a message and tried Angela again. Still no answer. At that point, Nina checked her watch and gasped. She hurried to the elevator, which took forever to arrive. Then it took twice as long as usual to find a cab, and once she did, traffic crawled through the rush-hour downpour.

By the time she'd taken off her wet things and dashed to the main rehearsal hall, almost everyone was there—everyone except Horst and Angela. Sylvia Kastle was the first to seek Nina out.

"The studio's buzzing with what happened at Angela's last night. And everyone knows you were there. How is she?"

"I tried calling her this morning," Nina said, thinking how many times this was going to happen today. "She didn't answer the phone. Last time I saw her she was understandably—upset."

"Tragic, just tragic," Sylvia murmured. "Some of the cast heard the report on the radio this morning, but the rest of us were shocked when Myrna made the announcement. So far, the weather seems to have kept the reporters away. I must say," she added, "the cast is very sympathetic. Everyone is ready to do whatever's necessary. Even Spence Sprague, our moody director-at-large, is prepared to treat Angela with kid gloves."

"If she shows up," Nina said. "Is Horst here?"

"No," Sylvia said, "and everyone is on pins and needles, wondering how he'll react when he learns the news . . . if he hasn't already."

Nina looked around and saw Tom Bell sitting in a corner hunched over his script. Sally Burman and Spence Sprague were in a huddle with Rafe and Robin. Brad Culver was going over lines with Noel Winston and Larry Spangler, the two "mature" character actors on the show. Robin saw Nina, and cornered her by the coffee machine as soon as she could tear herself away.

"Nina, I heard. It must have been *awful*," Robin said softly.

"Just be grateful you decided to go home when you did. It was a long night, and it's going to be an even longer day."

"Do the police have any leads at all?"

"Not really. It's much too soon for that."

"Angela must be a wreck."

"I wouldn't be surprised."

"You still have a lot to fill me in on, Nina—not that I want to get involved. Rafe has already warned me to stay out of this. But since I was at Jule's last night, I guess I won't be able to, will I?"

"Dino will probably want to ask you a few questions about what you saw and heard. But there's nothing you can tell him that I haven't, so . . ."

"Is Horst a suspect?" Robin whispered. "I thought maybe that's why he wasn't here. Nobody seems to know I went out with you and Angela last night, except Tom, and he didn't witness the fight between Horst and Evan, so I've kept my mouth shut about that little diversion."

"So have I, Robin," Nina admitted. "I didn't even tell Dino about it." Robin was surprised, but there was no time for her to pursue it further because at that very moment, Horst walked into the rehearsal hall, looking like seven miles of bad road. There were heavy circles under his eyes, his face was unshaven, and his clothes were rumpled.

"Morning, everyone," he said apologetically. "I know I'm late. There's no excuse for it, and I swear I'll be understanding the next time someone tells me they didn't hear their alarm go off. Let's get started, okay?" He looked around. "Where's Miss Dolan?"

No one moved. No one spoke. Horst looked at all their faces and knew immediately that something was wrong. He'd been avoiding Nina's gaze, but now he looked right at her. Nina took his arm and diplomatically led him out into the hall. Everyone remained silent as Nina closed the doors behind them.

"What's going on?" he asked.

"About last night, Horst . . . ," Nina began.

"Hey, Nina, I know I made an ass of myself last night, and I'm sorry. But surely everybody in there doesn't know about that. Or do they? What exactly did Angela say this morning?"

"She's not in yet, Horst. We don't know if she'll be coming in."

"Why not?"

"You don't know, do you?" Nina said, watching him closely.

"Know what?" Horst said, raising his voice.

Nina took a deep breath. "Evan Greer, the man you tried to pick a fight with last night, is dead. Angela found him in her town house about one this morning." Horst went white and his legs buckled. Nina tried to support him, but he waved her off and leaned heavily against the wall.

"My God," he muttered. "Oh, my God!" Nina thought he looked sincerely shocked. "Is Angela all right? What happened?"

"The only person Angela's been in touch with this morning is Helen, to explain things. As for Evan, the police are looking into it." If possible, Horst turned a shade paler. Then he started mumbling almost incoherently and massaging his temples with shaking hands.

"It was a mistake," he muttered, almost too softly for Nina to hear. "A mistake . . . I never should have . . ."

"Never should have *what*, Horst?" Nina said, a prickle of alarm coursing through her. "What is it?" She came over to him and gently placed a hand on his arm. He stared at her with glazed, bloodshot eyes.

"Nothing," he mumbled. "Nothing . . . forget it. Nina, please . . . don't get involved."

"I *am* involved, Horst. Are you?" His eyes grew wide, but Nina realized he wasn't looking at her. She turned and saw Angela coming down the hall, wearing a beige raincoat, matching rain hat, and dark glasses. A partially folded umbrella hung limply off her arm.

"Good morning, Nina," she said calmly. "Good morning, Horst." Nina wished she didn't have those damn glasses on so she could see her eyes. Horst hesitated, then went over to Angela and awkwardly held out his arms.

"I'm sorry, Angela. God, I'm sorry."

"So am I, Horst," she replied, her voice betraying her emotion. "So am I. About a lot of things." Then she stepped into his embrace. Nina felt she should probably make herself scarce, but she just couldn't.

"Nobody hurt your babies, did they, Angela? Molly Brown and the others—they're all right, aren't they?"

"Yes."

"It's going to be okay, Angela," Horst said soothingly. "Don't worry."

Nina strained to hear Angela's next few words. She wasn't sure, but they sounded like, "Don't *you* worry, either."

81

Nina virtually sleepwalked through the rest of the day. Her anxiety couldn't compensate for her lack of rest the night before. In spite of the gruesome shadow of murder that hung once again over the *Turning Seasons* family, the day went no more nor less smoothly than any other. As Sylvia had said, the cast and crew went out of their way to be professional and hardworking so that the final taping would be completed by 3:00 P.M. on the dot.

Helen arrived about halfway through the first rehearsal period. She looked older than her fifty-five years this morning. Her frosted blond hair was pulled severely back in a bun held in place by several tortoiseshell combs. Her silk suit was a somber shade of gray. Nina wondered if Helen felt any sympathy at all for Angela. After all, Helen had lost a husband to his own murderous son, and then a young lover to the police after he had killed two young women. She was running the Meyer Productions empire singlehandedly, but the strain was starting to show. Nina didn't envy her. Nina didn't like her, either, but then the feeling was mutual.

At the end of one rehearsed scene, Spence asked if Helen wished to speak to anyone. Helen didn't—she just wanted to make sure everything was in order. Then she left.

Angela and Horst stuck like glue to each other all day. They held hands. They talked. They whispered, almost conspiratorially. Everyone left them alone.

Back in her dressing room at last, an exhausted Nina took off her makeup and thanked God it was Friday. She was so tired she decided to stretch out on the divan for a while to rest and think. Her last thought before drowsing off was of how her reclining position resembled that of the wedding dress Jason had brought in—was it only yesterday?

Then the nightmare began.

Nina was in a hazy limbo, an endless space of darkness and shadows lit from an unknown source. The light was red, like blood, and it pulsated around her in shimmering pools. It felt heavy on her neck. She was searching for something or someone—what or whom, she didn't know. She just kept wandering, stumbling down a long, doorless corridor.

She heard a woman scream. It was Angela.

Nina started calling her name. It echoed in the stillness over and over and over. A cat yowled. Then another, then a third, until they became an unholy chorus of lamentation. Nina covered her ears with her hands, but she couldn't shut out the sound.

She ran on, now hearing male voices raised in argument. In the distance, she saw Horst and Evan fighting. Angela was trying to pry them apart. Nina tried to run to them, but her legs wouldn't work.

Suddenly Angela had the crystal vase of roses in her hands. She raised it high over her head and threw it at the two men with a shriek. It missed them, but continued to sail through the air in slow motion, a flurry of leaves and petals dancing in its wake. Too late, Nina realized she was directly in its path. She threw her hands up to her face for protection, and felt the impact of the glass, smelled the strong perfume of roses, crying out as the thorns tore at her flesh.

She experienced a sensation of falling. The floor seemed to be rising up to meet her. She was wet and covered with fragments of shattered glass and rose petals. There was a stabbing pain in her throat—the brooch! She yanked it free and heard the wedding dress rip. Part of the lace bodice dissolved, exposing her neck and breasts. She looked at the brooch in her hand. It was dripping with blood. She felt more blood trickle down from the wound at her throat and watched in horror as it stained the embroidery on the bodice and skirt. A man's hand grabbed her wrist.

She looked up into the deformed, leering face of Evan Greer.

Nina screamed.

Her eyes flew open, and she found herself staring into a man's eyes. He had a firm grip on both her hands. She started to struggle, then collapsed, realizing it was Dino.

"Nina, are you okay?" He was sitting on the edge of the divan, his curly hair glistening with raindrops. His coat and hands were wet, and tiny rivulets of water slid down the sleeves of his coat onto Nina's skin—the sensation she'd felt in her dream.

"I just stretched out for a second. . . . I must have fallen asleep. It was just a nightmare." *Just* a nightmare hardly seemed to describe the terror she had felt. Her heart was pounding and her hands still shook. "What are you doing here?"

"I wanted to talk to you and Ms. Dolan. The security guard out front said you hadn't left yet, so I came to look for you."

"Did you come up with something?"

"I came up with a lot of things," he said, his voice grim.

"Tell me!"

"Maybe *you'd* better tell *me* something first," Dino growled. He got up and shut the dressing room door.

"What's wrong?"

"Why didn't you tell me about the fight Greer almost got into with Krueger last night? About the threats Krueger made in front of a dozen witnesses?"

Nina swallowed. Dino was obviously angry.

"Tell me what you have first, Dino. Then I'll explain everything, I swear!"

Dino looked at her for a long, hard moment. "Estimated time of death is between twelve-thirty and one this morning. Aside from his face, there were no marks of violence on Greer's body. The lock on the back door that leads into the garden off the

84

kitchen was picked. The set of male prints we found are not Greer's. The M.E. checked his mouth—no sticky residue or signs that he'd been drinking that green booze. That means some other man was there; he must have worn gloves when he went in and out because he didn't leave any prints on the front door or the back. Greer's were only on the front, along with yours and Angela's. Hers were also on the crème de menthe bottle and a freshly washed rocks glass the boys found in one of the kitchen cabinets. What that means to me is Angela *knew* who else was there and was trying to destroy any evidence. I think you know who it was, too, Nina."

"I have suspicions, Dino, but my instincts tell me . . ."

"I don't deal in instincts. I deal in *facts*."

"How did you find out about the fight?" Nina asked nervously.

"I went to Jule's. Some guy named Devlin, the money taker at the front door, filled me in about it after I told him Greer was dead, and I asked if he had any ideas as to who might have done it. I also talked with the owner, Startoni. He didn't know anything about it."

"Did you talk to anyone else?"

"Everybody was clearing out by the time I got there. I did some checking into Greer's background." Dino scowled. "Maybe Angela should try computer dating next time."

"Why?"

"Oh, Greer's a honey of a guy. He had fingers in all kinds of muddy pies. Real unethical little side sports, but just legal enough to squeak by."

"Like what?"

"Favors, not in return for money, but for other favors. You need an escort? Call Greer. Want to organize a little side bet on the ponies or some pigskin? Call Greer. Real-estate deals, stock tips, drug

85

connections—name your poison. He was a walking *Yellow Pages* of vice. There'd been a few complaints filed against him by disgruntled 'patrons,' but no hard evidence to nail him. The people who depended on him surrounded him with a tight ring of protection. It worked both ways."

"Then a lot of people might have wanted to see him dead," Nina commented hopefully.

"Probably. Right now, though, I'm only interested in the one who was in Ms. Dolan's town house last night." Nina suddenly felt very uncomfortable under his steely gaze. "We have an eyewitness, too, by the way."

Nina looked up sharply. "To the murder?"

There was a knock on the door. Nina called out, "Come in," and Angela and Horst entered. Neither seemed surprised to see Rossi.

"The security guard told us you were looking for me," Angela said. "I thought I might find you in here. Horst insisted on doing all this now. Have you learned anything?"

"Yeah," Dino said laconically. He pulled a key out of his pocket. "For starters, we found this on Greer."

"It's the key to my town house. Anything else?"

"The usual. Wallet, ID, handkerchief . . . and this." Dino removed a small card from the breast pocket of his sportcoat and began to read out loud: "'Ah! May the red rose live alway To smile upon earth and sky! Why should the beautiful ever weep? Why should the beautiful die?' Mean anything to you? It's in Greer's handwriting."

"Yes," Angela said promptly. "That was the card Evan sent along with the roses he gave me. I left it in the bouquet."

"I guess you didn't miss it last night," Dino said.

"I did," Angela said, taking the card, "but . . ." Then suddenly she stopped.

"She thought I'd taken it, Lieutenant," Horst spoke up.

"Horst, *shut up!*" Angela hissed.

"We've talked it out all day, Angela," Horst said wearily. "I don't want to deny that I was there. It will only complicate things, right, Lieutenant?"

"Horst, no!" Angela pleaded, her eyes brimming with tears. She turned to Dino. "He didn't kill Evan. He *didn't!*"

"Were you involved in a fight at a club called Jule's last evening?" Dino asked.

"Yes," Horst replied. "I'd had too much to drink. I knew Angela was seeing somebody, and I knew where I'd find him. Angela went to Jule's a lot—I followed her there one night."

"Do you deny threatening to 'get him'? Or as someone at the club said, 'to know what he looks like so you can put your fist through his face the next time you saw him'?"

"No, I don't deny any of it," Horst answered, his voice barely audible. Angela went limp.

Dino stood up. "I think you'd better come down to the station with me, Mr. Krueger."

"Lieutenant," Nina quavered, feeling a need to say something. "Is that necessary?"

"I'm afraid so, Ms. McFall. We'll need a full statement and then proceed accordingly."

"No!" Angela cried. "He didn't *do* anything!"

Dino turned to Horst. "Let's go."

"I'm going with you," Angela insisted.

"No," Horst said softly. "I just want to get this over with, and I don't want you involved."

"But you didn't kill him!" Angela wailed.

"Truth is," Horst said, "I might have. I honestly don't remember."

Chapter Six

"Horst came to apologize," Angela said about an hour later as she paced distractedly around Nina's living room. It was clear to Nina that Angela needed to talk, so she'd invited her to the penthouse after Rossi had taken Horst downtown.

Nina sat down on the sofa and poured them each a cup of herbal tea, asking, "How did he get in?"

"He thought I'd be home early, since I had to work the next day. He went to another bar after those two *animals* threw him out of Jule's. He kept drinking, he told me at lunch, and thinking about how he'd embarrassed me in front of everyone. He wanted to tell me how sorry he was and then bow out graciously. Evan let him in."

"What?" Nina said, surprised.

"Horst rang the bell. Evan answered and invited him in. They went into the living room. Evan told Horst to help himself to a drink. Horst did. They sat and talked—or at least Evan did. Horst sat and drank."

"Then Evan was early?"

"He must have been. Odd, because he'd never done that before."

"Then what?" Nina asked.

"Horst changed his mind. He got ready to leave. But Evan insisted on showing him around."

"This doesn't make sense, Angela! Why would Evan do that if he knew you were coming at one?"

"I don't know. But it wasn't a good idea. Horst had never seen the place, and being given the grand tour by Evan only flooded his poor mind with images of Evan and me there in . . . intimate moments. Horst's mind was dulled by alcohol—the rest really isn't clear in his head. By the time they reached the parlor, Horst was definitely feeling hostile. To the best of Horst's recollection, Evan seemed determined to have him stay, almost as if he were rubbing his nose in our affair. Horst had had enough. He turned to go, and Even grabbed him by the arm. Horst swung, hit Evan in the face, and left through the front door. He barely remembers getting home."

Nina was growing more puzzled by the minute. "Did Horst say anything else about Evan's behavior?"

"Like what?"

"I don't know—like how he was acting when Horst first came in."

Angela thought a moment then said, "Horst *did* say Evan didn't answer the bell right away. It was only after Horst pounded on the door and started calling my name that he eventually let him in."

"Almost as though he was expecting someone else, someone he didn't want to see," Nina thought out loud.

"Who?"

"Maybe the murderer. Maybe Evan insisted that Horst stay because he didn't want to be left alone. Maybe he was afraid."

"That doesn't sound like Evan. But if everything you say Detective Rossi found out about Evan is true,

I'm hardly an expert on what Evan was like. He talked me into buying that town house, you know. I imagine his palm was favorably greased in some way for it." Angela sighed. "Obviously, he was an extremely clever, cunning man."

"But not clever enough to keep from being killed," Nina muttered.

"You're on our side in this, mine and Horst's, aren't you, Nina?" Angela asked anxiously.

"Of course I am. No matter how drunk Horst was, I still can't believe he could kill anyone." Nina paused to mull over some facts, then asked, "Where was Evan's topcoat? I never saw it."

"The police found it thrown over a chair in the den."

"Where *is* the den exactly?" Nina asked.

"On the ground floor. You wouldn't have noticed it—the lights were out."

"Odd. I would think if Evan had planned on staying, he would have hung his coat in a closet. I imagine it was very expensive."

"Very. A blue cashmere Ferre."

"Then why leave it where your cats might shed all over it? Besides, the killer might have been there in the dark, watching and ready to make a hasty reteat if the wrong person showed. And that means whoever killed Evan had to know where he was going, and where you lived."

Angela frowned. "That narrows it down considerably. I've only been at that address for little more than a week. I have an unlisted phone number. Horst knew my address from the office, but no one else at the studio even *knew* Evan."

"At least not that we know of," Nina replied. Chessy rubbed against Angela's legs, and she bent down to stroke him while Nina went over in her mind everything Angela and Dino had explained so far.

90

"There's one thing I don't understand at all," Nina said, brows furrowed in thought. "The card Evan sent with the roses—why would he have put it in his pocket?"

"I don't have a clue," Angela sighed, finally sitting down to try the tea. "It's cold," she pronounced and promptly set the cup back down.

"The card," Nina said suddenly. "Do you still have it?"

"Right here," Angela said, removing it from her purse. "Why?"

Nina took the card and scanned it. "How much did you tell Evan about my—involvement with the other murders?"

"Just what I told you last night—that you liked a puzzle, you often stumbled across an occasional clue, and you helped the police."

"Then," Nina conjectured, "maybe Evan thought that if something happened to him in your home, I might be involved. Maybe he put this in his pocket as a clue! I was there, remember, when you told him you tucked the card in with the flowers so you could always see it."

"Nina, darling, really," Angela scoffed. "You're awfully full of yourself. It's not attractive. And it's not helpful. If Evan were afraid he was going to die, I seriously doubt that *you'd* be on his mind." She checked her watch. "I wish that damn lawyer I called to represent Horst at the precinct would call! What's taking so long?"

Nina kept staring at the words on the card: "Ah! May the red rose live alway. To smile upon earth and sky! Why should the beautiful ever weep? Why should the beautiful die?"

"Did Evan ever give you flowers before?" she asked.

"Of course."

"Did they always come with cards?"

"Yes, but he'd never written anything quite so romantic as this one."

"Romantic—yes," Nina mused. "I remember the birthday toast he made to you. It wasn't exactly the most clever, original thing I've ever heard."

"Are you trying to make a point?" Angela asked, growing more fidgety by the minute.

"Yes. I don't think Evan made this up. I think he'd either heard or read it somewhere. Do you recognize it?"

"No."

"Was there anything special about the roses themselves?"

"They're Baccharat roses. Exceptionally long stems. A deep red color. The center is almost black— some people call it the black rose. Really, Nina," Angela said petulantly, "this is getting us nowhere."

Maybe and maybe not, Nina thought. But she was sure that Evan had chosen that quotation for a reason. Baccharat roses . . . Nina was reminded of her nightmare. The roses flying at her; the brooch stabbing her—the brooch! It was still in her purse. Funny, neither Jason nor Dennis had come looking for it. But then, they didn't know Angela had returned it to Nina.

"I can't stay any longer, Nina. I'm going down to the station," Angela said, rising to her feet.

"Maybe that's not such a good idea. . . ."

"I don't care! Horst wouldn't be in this mess if it wasn't for me."

"He might be in *less* of a mess if you hadn't tried to cover for him," Nina pointed out.

"I just panicked when I saw that glass and the liqueur bottle. I replaced the bottle, but there was still some creme de menthe left in the glass. When you walked in, I tried to cover it up by adding brandy and drinking it down—one of the most revolting taste experiences of my life! *Damn* Horst! I mean, *nobody* drinks creme de menthe anymore, but those were some of the things about Horst I liked—his tenacious habits and standards. His predictability. I always knew what to expect from him." Angela moved to the window, staring out a moment, then added, "I couldn't just stand by last night, and I can't now. I know Horst didn't kill Evan. And if the police don't believe that, then damn it, *I'll* find out who really did!"

"Angela, wait a minute!" Nina said in alarm. But Angela had already grabbed her rain gear and swept out the door.

The waiting eventually got to Nina, too, as the rain finally lessened and the sky began to clear, several hours after Angela's departure. Dino hadn't called. She knew he was upset with her for not telling him about Horst's attack on Evan, and she wished now that she had. Two people had tried to cover up for Horst now, and that made it look as if they were protecting him for a reason. Nina had done so because she thought he was innocent. But she wondered if Angela's actions had been for the same reason. Angela and Horst had had the whole day to talk.

A whole day to make up a good story?

No, Nina didn't believe that. She remembered Horst asking about Molly Brown. It seemed that Angela's cats liked him and Evan. Nina hadn't seen any of them for a while after she'd entered Angela's town house, and, according to Angela, they only hid when there was a stranger in the house. So there must have been someone unknown to them in Angela's house last night.

Nina thought back over the events at Jule's. And then it came to her—the phone messages for Evan that Jay had delivered. The party had called several times and Evan hadn't called back. The caller threatened to make an appearance if Evan didn't contact him . . . or her. Evan had looked uncomfortable and excused himself. Did he make that call? If not, did the person show up? Could it have been the blonde?

Well, there was only one way to find out. Nina was tired, but she began to dress for another night on the town.

It was about eight o'clock when Nina arrived at Jule's. This time, there was no one waiting in line to get in. The man with the beard wasn't on guard at the door, either. Instead, it was the dark-haired man, Devlin, whom Dino had questioned. He recognized Nina immediately and smiled.

"Where's your friend tonight?" she asked nonchalantly. Devlin looked puzzled. "The man with the beard."

"Oh. He didn't come in tonight."

"I hope he's all right," Nina said, hoping to get him to open up. "I mean, that man last night did hit him pretty hard."

"He can take it," Devlin responded.

Nina decided she had to be more direct. "You know, something's been nagging at me."

"What's that?"

"He looked so familiar to me. And he seemed to recognize me, too. I've been trying to place him all day. I didn't catch his name last night."

"Buck," Devlin said.

No bells went off in Nina's head. "Is it a nickname?"

Devlin met her gaze. "Don't know. He called himself Buck when he first came here. That's all I needed to know. Sometimes the less you know, the better." His eyes bored into hers, and Nina felt a distinct chill.

"Well, thank you. I guess he just has one of those faces." Nina smiled. She didn't get one back.

Nina checked her coat and moved through the double doors into the foyer. It was as grand as she remembered. Idly, she wondered what this place must have been like in its heyday. What kind of people had once walked up and down this marble staircase? And where were they now, those men and women in their frock coats and ball gowns?

When she reached the top of the stairs, Nina found herself drawn to the roped-off stairway that led to the third floor. It triggered an uncontrollable desire to know what lay beyond, but she resisted the temptation to sneak up the steps, rationalizing that it had nothing to do with what she was here for. She turned and headed instead for the main barroom.

The drapes parted before she got to them and Dominic Startoni appeared, impeccably dressed in a navy pin-striped suit.

"Nina McFall, right?"

"Yes," Nina responded with a warm smile. She extended her hand. He shook it gallantly, then held it for a moment as she went on, "I'm sorry about Mr. Greer."

"Yes. A shock. A tragedy. He'll be missed. I couldn't believe it when the police came and told me. Poor Miss Dolan must be . . . well, I guess there just aren't any words."

Nina saw Dominic's eyes mist. Was it possible he didn't know the unsavory side of Evan Greer's character?

"Had you known him long?" Nina asked, all sympathy.

"No, but I liked him. He did his job well. We weren't close, but it's a terrible thing when any life is taken."

"I agree," Nina said.

"I got the impression that the police have a lead—the man I hear threatened Evan last night."

"Well, I happen to know that man," Nina said quickly. "Angela does, too, and neither of us believes he's guilty. I'm sure the police will eventually discover that for themselves."

"Are you here alone?" Startoni asked, scrutinizing her.

"Yes, actually."

"A terrible waste. I was on my way upstairs to have dinner. Would you consider joining me?"

If anyone could give Nina information about Evan, Dominic Startoni could. And he'd said the magic word—"upstairs."

"I'd like that very much," Nina replied. "I wasn't looking forward to eating alone."

"Then it's done! Come with me."

He escorted her across the balcony, unclasped the red velvet rope, and let Nina go ahead of him up the stairs. Soon they were on the third floor. Nina followed Dominic down a long hallway with oak panels and red flocked wallpaper. Dominic hesitated in front of one door.

"That was Evan's office. I haven't gone in—the police asked me to make sure nothing was disturbed, so I've stayed away." No sooner had he spoken than the door opened and a very startled Jay faced Nina and Dominic, whose face immediately darkened. "What were you doing in there?" he demanded.

Jay was obviously uncomfortable. "I—I needed some of Evan's files to do a liquor inventory."

"I gave instructions that *no one* was to go in there. The police . . ."

"I know all that," Jay responded defensively. "I didn't touch anything I didn't have to. This place still has to be kept running, you know. Excuse me." Jay locked the door, moved quickly between them, and hurried down the stairs.

"Sorry for the outburst, Ms. McFall," Startoni said. "It was just the shock of seeing the door open—I half expected to see Evan. Jay's right, the show must go on, and he's responsible enough not to muck with anything he shouldn't."

"I understand," Nina said. "And if we're going to be sharing dinner, please call me Nina."

"All right, Nina. And I'm Dominic." He led her to the end of the hall and opened the last door, stepping back to allow Nina to enter the room first. She saw that the Victorian theme was repeated here as well. It was a comfortable sitting room, in shades of crimson and soft green. The furnishings were all period pieces, right down to the lighting fixtures. Two Morris chairs, a small table between them, faced an ornate marble fireplace flanked by floor-to-ceiling bookcases. Nina was drawn to the cozy setting and warmed herself in front of the fire that burned cheerily behind two huge andirons.

"March is a bitter month," Dominic commented. "It teases you with the promise of spring but breaks that promise again and again."

"I didn't get the chance to tell you last night how wonderful I think this place is," Nina offered.

"Thanks. A lot of sweat and love went into Jule's."

"It's like a shrine to older and better days," she added.

He looked at her quizzically. "That's exactly what it was meant to be. Would you like a glass of sherry?"

"Yes, thanks." Nina looked around the room as Dominic poured two drinks. He didn't fit in here somehow, and watching him, she noticed he looked uncomfortable in the surroundings. It was as if he were trying to prevent his rough edges from damaging the softness and gentility of the decor.

"Was the Victorian theme of Jule's your idea?" she asked.

"Yes," he answered. "Why?"

"Just curious."

"You don't think it's my style, right?" he asked, smiling.

"Maybe something like that," Nina admitted. Dominic held out her glass of sherry, and she noticed how fragile the delicate crystal looked in his large, hairy hand. She also noticed a wedding band. He caught her look as she took the drink.

"It *is* a wedding band, Nina," he said. "But I am alone now. My wife . . . left me, quite some time back." By the way he phrased it, Nina couldn't tell if his wife had walked out on him or died.

"I'm sorry," she said.

"So, Nina, why are you really here?" Dominic asked abruptly.

Surprised, Nina said, "What do you mean?"

"You're not the type of woman to go out for dinner the night after her friend's lover was found murdered."

"You're right," Nina admitted. "I was just hoping to . . ."

"To find some answers?"

"Yes."

"Sit," he offered, indicating one of the Morris chairs. Nina sank into it as Dominic settled into its twin. "I'd like answers, too, but I don't think the police would like the idea of *either* of us trying to do their job for them."

That's putting it mildly, Nina thought wryly. If Dino knew she was here . . .

"What do you want to ask me?" Dominic said.

Nina began by asking him if he knew if Evan Greer had been involved in anything unethical on the side.

"If he was, I didn't know anything about it. Evan was an odd man. He kept to himself. I do, too, so we got along well. I guess we all have our little quirks, our secrets—some more serious than others. The one thing I did talk to him about once was his . . . choice of women. That's why I was very pleased when he started seeing your friend."

"What exactly do you mean?" Nina asked, remembering the blonde.

"To be blunt, Evan went for cheap women, the younger and gaudier, the better. I think Angela changed all that."

"I noticed a young blond woman here last night. I saw her watching Angela and Evan together, and she didn't look happy about it. She also seemed to—well, fit your description of Evan's taste. You don't happen to know her, do you?"

"I don't believe so," Dominic said.

"She seemed to know you. I was looking up the staircase to this floor and she warned me that you didn't like people snooping around."

"*Now* I know who you mean. Her name's Rose—although she doesn't do a damn bit of justice to her namesake. She hung around a lot."

Rose! Could Evan have been accusing her by confiscating the card from Angela's bouquet? "Do you know her last name?" Nina asked eagerly.

Dominic shook his head.

"Sorry. Why?"

"She might know something that could help the police."

"Or she could have killed him," Dominic stated calmly. The phone rang, and Dominic answered with a trace of annoyance. "When? All right, I'll be right down." He hung up and turned apologetically to Nina. "I'm terribly sorry. Will you take a raincheck for dinner? Something has come up. . . ."

"Of course," Nina said, fervently wishing they could have talked further.

"But please stay. Have dinner downstairs, on me. I won't take no for an answer."

Nina was famished—she'd had nothing but tea all day. "All right. I will."

"Good. If I can, I'll join you. This may not take long."

They went back downstairs and Dominic led her into the dining room. Nina noticed that Jay was nowhere in sight. Dominic seated her in a secluded corner, signaled a waiter, and told him to give Nina the red-carpet treatment. The waiter bowed and glided off. Before Dominic turned to leave, he became very serious.

"Nina," he said quietly, "be careful. You came in here with suspicions about Evan. Now you have suspicions about this woman he might have been seeing. Murder is a dangerous thing to play games with, especially for somebody with no experience—*capisce*?"

"Yes, Dominic," Nina assured him gravely, wondering how he'd react if he only knew *half* the experience she'd had with murder!

"Good." He smiled, gave her a wink, and left the room. Nina couldn't wait to call Dino and tell him about Rose, then decided she really didn't have anything to say. He'd scoff at her theory that Evan had tried to give whoever found his body a clue. No, before she called Dino, she'd need some more information. She decided to eat, and was looking over the menu when Jay sat down at her table.

"Hi, Ms. McFall," he said. His dazzling smile looked somehow forced.

"Hello, Jay. I was hoping to find you down here. Mr. Startoni invited me to join him for dinner, but he had some emergency or other, so here I am. What do you recommend?"

"That you tell Ms. Dolan to be careful," Jay responded in a whisper.

100

Nina stared at him. "What?"

Jay lowered his voice to such a confidential tone that Nina had to put her head close to his in order to hear him.

"Evan Greer was scum. He was up to his filthy ears in every racket in town."

"How do you know?" Nina asked.

"I have eyes and ears. People talk. Nobody pays much attention to a bartender."

"Did you ever tell Mr. Startoni?"

"Yeah. But I didn't have any proof. Dom's too trusting. He wants to believe there's good in everybody. Greer ran this club well. I never saw him cheat Dom in any way, and that became a perfect character reference to allow him to pull crap on the side—shady deals with some of the customers."

Nina frowned. "What does this have to do with Angela?"

"Nothing, except for the fact that she was involved with him. Whoever killed Greer probably wanted to shut his mouth about something. They might think Ms. Dolan knows too much. She should lie low someplace, maybe move in with somebody until the police get the killer."

"What do you know about a woman named Rose?" Nina asked abruptly.

"How do *you* know about her?" Jay asked, surprised.

Nina explained talking to the blonde and then seeing her with Greer. "Dominic said her name was Rose."

"Yeah—Rose something-or-other. She did 'favors' for Greer, entertained his out-of-town friends. But she was hung up on him. She didn't care too much for your friend. Greer had been sending her out on more 'calls,' spending less time with her himself. But that's how Greer was. Rose wasn't the first piece of

101

merchandise he sweet-talked into a few months of fun and games. His friends liked variety."

The waiter approached the table and Nina said she needed more time to make up her mind before ordering. Once he was gone, Jay continued quietly, "Rose is a tough one. She doesn't give up that easy. She also has a bad temper. I'm pretty sure Greer was ready to give her walking papers."

"Why do you think Evan was seeing Angela?" Nina asked now. "I don't mean that as any kind of put-down to her. It's just that Evan Greer seems to have been a manipulator, a user. What did he hope to get out of her?"

"It's funny," Jay reflected. "I think he really liked Ms. Dolan, at least as much as he was capable of liking anybody. And she makes big bucks. That made her a pigeon—two for the price of one. Who knows what he thought he could get out of her? There was that town house he talked her into buying. I'm sure he got a piece of that action somehow. I noticed that she always wore a lot of expensive jewelry when she came in here, and I'm sure Greer noticed it, too. Look at the way she was decked out last night."

"The brooch? That's just a prop," Nina said, "a piece of costume jewelry for the show. Angela borrowed it to wear for the evening, like she did a lot of jewelry and clothes. I've done it on occassion myself. I don't have a good eye when it comes to gems, but Evan certainly should have known a fake when he saw one."

Jay shrugged. "Well, I guess we'll never know what he wanted."

"What about those telephone calls for Evan last night? Was it a man or a woman calling? Could it have been Rose, is what I'm asking," Nina said.

"No, it was a man. Deep voice. Angry voice."

"Did he leave his name?"

"No."

"What about a number?"

"Yeah. I wrote it down on the messages I took."

"Are they still around, or could you remember the number?" Nina asked with hopeful urgency.

"A bust on both counts. I take so many numbers over the phone that I forget 'em as soon as I write 'em down. And Greer always picked up the message slips. He never left anything hanging around for too long."

"Could they still be in his office?"

Jay hesitated. "They might, if he didn't throw them out." He met Nina's beseeching gaze and said firmly, "I know what you're asking, Ms. McFall, but I already got chewed out for being in there once tonight. Anyway, I don't think you should get mixed up in this. I've probably told you too much as it is. I only did it so you could warn Ms. Dolan."

"Have you told the police any of this?"

"I'd already left last night when they got there, but I will if you think it'll help"

"I think it would," said a voice near them. Nina jumped and looked up—to see Dino. He scowled at her, then directed his attention to Jay. "Lieutenant Rossi, NYPD. Are you Jay Benedict?"

"Yes." Jay looked very worried.

"I'd like to ask you a few questions—if you're not all talked out." Nina got the point but didn't react.

"No," Jay said. "I just have to make a quick round of the place—Mr. Startoni put me in charge of covering some of Mr. Greer's bases tonight. I'll be right back. Good to see you again, Ms. McFall. By the way, I've done some thinking about what you said last night, and I just might take you up on your offer."

Nina saw Dino raise an eyebrow at this. "Good," she said without explanation. Jay moved off.

"Work fast, don't you, lady?" Dino growled as he joined her at the table.

Refusing to rise to the bait, Nina asked a question of her own. "What happened with Horst?"

"His prints match those found in the town house. No surprise there after his confession. And there's that eyewitness, a lady across the street who ID's Krueger as the man she saw leaving Ms. Dolan's place at about twelve forty-five."

"Horst did *not* kill Evan Greer," Nina said emphatically. "I don't care how bad it looks!"

Dino looked into her blazing green eyes. "Easy," he said. "I'm inclined to agree with you, for once. But to my superiors it looks like a classic 'crime of passion' thing. Angela didn't help by trying to tidy up after Krueger—she could have erased valuable clues. I'll come down on *you* later for withholding the fact that Krueger tried to mess Greer up in here last night."

"Where's Horst now?"

"Krueger's released, thanks to the lawyer Ms. Dolan set him up with. The three of them left in a whispering huddle."

"Angela said that Horst admitted to punching Evan in the face. Is there any possibility he could have killed him accidentally?"

"It's possible. Million to one, but it's possible."

"Maybe the real killer came in after Horst hit him and saw the bruises as an opportunity to cover up his own method," Nina suggested.

"*If* there was somebody else there." Nina glared at him, but Dino didn't give her a chance to object. "I have to play devil's advocate, Nina. There's no hard evidence to establish there was anybody else in there but Krueger and Greer. Sure, the killer could have worn gloves. He could have picked the lock and come in. All 'coulds,' Nina. But a smart attorney 'could' convince a jury that *Krueger* picked that lock, that he wasn't thinking too clearly because he'd been drinking, and left some prints."

"What do you mean, a smart attorney? Horst hasn't been arrested."

"Not yet. But if we don't come up with another suspect and a good motive or two, the D.A.'s office will push for an arrest."

"There's got to be something we can do!" Nina said.

"Whoa! When I said 'we,' I meant the police."

"Well, I've already come up with some very interesting leads. If you're not interested in hearing them, Detective . . ."

"I didn't say that. Jesus, Nina, we've been over this ground so many times! I'm not even going to say anything this time. But I *do* expect you to be very careful. You seem to have a nice thing going with the bartender. Use it. But I don't want to hear anything he told you until *I'm* done asking questions. We'll compare notes later at your place—if that's all right with you?"

"I think it's a wonderful idea, Lieutenant," Nina said demurely. "Maybe I'll just sacrifice the fine cuisine here and make us a late supper—if that's all right with *you*."

Rossi smiled. Nina couldn't wait to get home.

Home. She turned the word over in her mind the way one would savor a delicious Godiva chocolate. Nina still hadn't quite gotten used to her luxurious penthouse apartment. Neither had Dino, but tonight she hoped they might both be able to relax and enjoy it.

It was about nine-thirty when the cab Nina had hailed outside Jule's was nearing Primrose Towers. Nina felt she'd accomplished quite a bit tonight. She had one strong lead in Rose, and a possible second in whoever made those phone calls to Evan. She'd also wangled some time alone with Dino. Remembering she needed a few things for dinner, Nina changed her mind at the last minute and instructed the driver to drop her off in front of a gourmet food emporium and caterer instead of taking her directly home.

The streets weren't as crowded as Nina had expected—the cold and damp were obviously keeping everybody indoors. Then, too, it wasn't that late. Give Broadway an hour or two more and it would be thronged with a whole menagerie of party animals.

Nina had made her purchases and was walking toward West End Avenue when she saw the couple come out of a small bar.

The woman was blond, dressed in tight designer jeans, a fur jacket, and high heels. The man, who had his back to Nina, wore a shearling coat and cowboy boots. Nina could see long blond hair curling over the top of his coat collar. They were obviously having a bitter argument. The woman started to run away from the man, but he grabbed her savagely by the arm and threw her up against the wall. That's when Nina recognized both of them—Rose and Buck, the bouncer.

Nina froze as Rose saw her and reacted sharply. Buck turned, immediately released his grip on the woman, and broke into a run. But he wasn't running away. He was headed straight for Nina!

Chapter Seven

Nina dropped her groceries and ran. She knew she didn't have a prayer of outdistancing Buck for long, so she dashed back toward the lights of Broadway, adrenaline flooding her veins with the hope of safety in numbers. She could hear his heavy steps behind her, but she was too afraid to look back and see how close he was. None of the few passersby paid any attention to either Nina or her pursuer.

She rounded the corner and ducked into the first open store she came to. It was a small grocery with only two cramped aisles. There were no customers. Nina didn't even see a clerk.

She chanced a quick look through the glass door. One or two people passed by, but there was no sign of Buck. Nina edged her way into the back, hoping there might be a rear exit. Instead, she found the clerk, unpacking cartons of canned vegetables.

"Do you have a telephone?" Nina gasped. "I have to make an important call." The clerk, a brawny, sweat-stained Hispanic in his forties, looked at her with no comprehension. "*Teléfono?*" Nina tried again.

"Sí," he said gruffly, light dawning. *"Dos cuadras, al norte."* He waved his hand in the direction of the street.

"No, not out there," Nina said, trying to be calm. "In here. *Teléfono. ¡Policía!"* Something must have clicked at the mention of the law.

"¿Policía?" he repeated. Nina nodded. Her look of fright and furtive glances at the door got her point across.

"Sì, señora! Ven acá." He then led her around a beer display and into a dingy back room curtained off by makeshift drapes on a wooden rod. There was very little light and Nina could barely see anything around her. Somewhere a radio played muted Spanish music. *"El teléfono aquí. Esperare!"* Nina didn't understand him, but he held up a comforting hand, then mimed locking the door.

"Thank you—I mean, *gracias,"* Nina mumbled, still trying to catch her breath. The clerk went out. Nina fumbled with the standard black phone. She had to get in touch with Dino, who she assumed must still be at Jule's. Since she didn't know the number and didn't want to waste time dialing Information, she dialed Dino's office instead. It seemed to take forever on the rotary phone.

"Sergeant Harper, please. It's an emergency!"

"Just one moment, please," an official voice droned. As she was put on hold, Nina realized she probably should have dialed 911. She peered through the crack in the curtains. There was no sound and no sign of the clerk.

"Sergeant Harper. May I help you?"

"Charley, it's Nina McFall. I'm in a jam. I need . . ." Nina's voice caught in her throat when she heard a sudden crash and the distinctive clamor of rolling cans. My God, Nina silently gasped, he's already inside! She dropped the receiver, faintly hearing Charley call her name and ask if she was all right. Nina's eyes, adjusted now to the darkened area, saw a door leading to what she prayed was safety. Her only problem was having to cross in front of the curtained doorway. The store was deathly quiet.

An obstacle course of cartons and cans loomed up in shadowy columns. She crept stealthily behind one of them. She couldn't see into the market now, but if Buck came in, the spill of light from the opened drapes would give his entrance away. Nina held her breath.

Panic-marked seconds dragged by. Nina heard something snap under a footfall. Then the glimmer of light between the curtains vanished, blocked by someone standing directly in front of them.

Nina heard Buck rip the material off the rod and charge in. With all her strength, Nina pushed the nearest stack of cartons. She heard Buck swear in surprise, then a dull thud and a groan. Nina didn't waste another second. She ran to the back door and threw all her weight against the bar. It opened, tumbling her into an alley. She slammed the door shut tight and hastily shoved an empty metal trash can in front of it. It might not stop him, she thought, but it might slow him down a little.

Nina was out of the alley and back onto the cross street now. She heard nothing behind her, and flattened herself against the brick wall of a building to fill her burning lungs. Then, with trembling legs, she ran on. She didn't feel safe until the lights of Primrose Towers beckoned to her like a beacon.

Looking neither right nor left, she sped on. She had just mounted the curb when the shadowy figure of a man leapt out of a car and grabbed her arm. Nina screamed, whirled around, and found herself staring into the concerned eyes of Dino Rossi. Shaking all over, she clung to him.

"Nina, what happened? Charley caught me just

before I left Jule's. He said you were in trouble but he didn't know where you were calling from. I got here as quick as I could."

"Just take me inside, please," Nina said with her last few ounces of air. "I'll explain."

The doorman, Willy, dashed out a moment later. Dino thanked him for having watchful eyes, told him everything was okay, and accompanied a sagging Nina to the elevator and up to her penthouse.

Chessy, who'd been asleep in his favorite chair, opened one sleepy eye. Sensing that Nina was in good hands, he curled himself into a tight ball and went back to sleep. Dino gave Nina a glass of brandy, sat her down, and listened to her story.

"You told me last night that this guy looked familiar to you," Dino said when she had finished. "Do you have any ideas yet about where you might know him from?"

"No," Nina whispered.

"I made a list of everybody who was working at the club last night. I didn't like the gut feeling I had when I learned that your friend didn't bother to show up tonight, didn't call in or anything. The bartender said his real name is Wes Timmins. Greer hired him. They were tight. The boys are running a check on him."

"The name *is* familiar," Nina said, "but . . ."

"It's okay," he said softly, kneeling in front of her. "Don't worry about it now. Just try to relax." He gently tilted her head back by placing a finger underneath her chin. She looked into his eyes. "You didn't ask for this one, babe. You just walked right into it." He wrapped his fingers gently around hers. It never ceased to amaze Nina how his tough, commanding body was capable of such tenderness. "I gotta make a call. Sit tight."

Dino phoned Charley and asked him to send a car over to the market, adding that there wasn't much

110

chance that Timmins was still there, but somebody should check on the clerk. He also wanted someone to stake out Timmins's apartment and hail him when he came home. There was also the matter of the woman, Rose, to look into. Nina could see that Dino had a busy night ahead of him, and it wouldn't include her.

He said he'd see Charley in a few minutes, hung up, and joined Nina on the sofa.

"So much for dinner?" Nina asked, already knowing the answer.

"Sorry. Seems like I say that a lot, don't I?"

"It's all right," Nina replied softly.

"No, it's not, Nina. I'm a cop. It's my job to pick up on clues, and I've been picking up a lot from you lately. There's a distance between us and it doesn't take Columbo to figure out what's on both our minds. I knew you wanted space, and I knew why."

"Dino . . ."

"No, just shut that pretty mouth and let me get this out. It's not easy." He got up and, nervously sticking his hands in his pockets, moved to the windows. "I've been seeing the same look in your eyes that I used to see in my wife's. Believe me, that's the only comparison between the two of you I'm ever gonna make, but I know what that look means. If I was late or didn't call her, she thought the worst. She kept wondering how she'd deal with it if she ever *did* get that call. Every morning when she made the bed, she wondered if we'd made love for the last time. I guess maybe that's what drove her to sleep with other guys. She fantasized about hearing a sympathetic voice on the phone saying that I . . ."

"Stop it, Dino, please!" Nina cried, getting up and rushing over to him. She circled her arms around his waist and leaned against his broad back. "Yes, I *have* had those thoughts. I can't help it. The thought of losing what we have, losing you . . . it makes me hurt so much inside." Dino turned but kept her at arm's length.

"Nobody's blaming you. But maybe it's something we have to straighten out."

"Maybe it is," Nina replied almost inaudibly. There was a long look between them, then Dino pulled her into his arms, their lips hungrily devouring each other.

It was a long time before they parted. "God, you feel good," he uttered huskily. Then he held her close again and buried his face in her hair. Nina couldn't resist the warmth that flooded her body. Gently but purposefully, she eased his jacket off his shoulders. As he kissed her neck, she began to undo his tie and shirt buttons. Her fingers found the curly mat of hair that blossomed over his rock-hard chest, and she felt Dino's nimble hands slip her silk blouse from her skirt and sweep underneath, running their rough palms against the velvet skin of her back. Their breathing became harsher, and Nina's heart echoed the urgent pounding of Dino's against her breast.

Suddenly he stopped and pulled away from her like a moth too close to a desirable flame. Nina closed her eyes, fighting the resentment that threatened to overwhelm her. She knew what was coming—she'd known it when Dino made his call to Charley—and she had to accept it. When she opened her eyes, Dino had already scooped up his jacket and was heading for the door. He said nothing as he grabbed his trench coat and reached for the doorknob. But he didn't open the door.

"I hate it, too," he said, without turning.

"It's . . . not like I didn't expect it," she replied. Then he turned to her, his gray eyes still lit by passion. His tie was undone, his shirt still unbuttoned, and his chest still heaved with pain and longing.

"I love you," he said simply.

112

"I know you do," Nina replied without moving. She knew if she took one single step, she'd fling herself at him and beg him to stay. "I love you, too."

"I won't say I'm sorry again tonight. It's just a word. It doesn't really help take the edge off the guilt I'm feeling, or dampen what I felt in your arms. It's just a word."

Nina nodded, and Dino quickly turned and yanked at the doorknob so hard she was afraid he'd rip it off. He opened the door and stood staring into the hall for a moment. Then he slammed it shut, threw his coat down on the chair and strode to the phone. He punched out several numbers, waiting impatiently.

"Charley, it's Dino. I was officially off duty an hour ago. You guys get anything, call me at Ms. McFall's number. It's in my book. I'll be here longer than I expected." He hung up and turned to Nina with a sudden boyish grin. "Don't ever say I never gave you top billing!"

Nina, choked with emotion, ran into his arms.

And later, when she sleepily felt him stealing one last kiss and heard him slip out of the bedroom, she blissfully turned over and dreamed of being in his arms again. . . .

Chapter Eight

Nina woke up late on Saturday, and she was famished. She yawned and stretched, then turned over to see Chessy lounging on the side of the bed that Dino had occupied just a few hours ago. She rolled over, letting the sheets slide off her shapely legs, and scratched behind the cat's ears. He closed his eyes, purred loudly, then squirmed over on his back. Nina obliged him by rubbing his stomach.

She took a shower, put on some coffee, and checked the refrigerator for breakfast food. The shelves were almost bare. She settled for a day-old grapefruit half, then splurged on two pieces of buttered toast, smothered in marmalade—she'd work the extra calories off later. It occurred to her that she'd worked off quite a few last night, and she wasn't thinking only about her night with Dino.

Who was Wes "Buck" Timmins? Who was Rose? And how were they connected? Dino had said Evan and Buck were tight. If they had been tight enough, Buck might have known things he shouldn't—and vice versa. Maybe Buck and Rose were having a thing on the side and Evan tried to interfere? Maybe a lot of things. She had meant to ask Dino if what had happened last night would remove enough suspicion from Horst to avoid an arrest. She doubted it.

The phone jolted Nina out of her thoughts. She answered and smiled, recognizing Dino's voice.

"Hi, babe. How you feeling this morning?"

"All things considered, very good," Nina purred. "Thank you for last night, darling. You do know how to make a girl feel wanted."

"Believe me, it was my pleasure. I haven't got too long, but I wanted to fill you in on a few things. First, that clerk in the grocery store is okay. His head's gonna ache for a little while, though. Timmins chopped him in the neck. Karate-chopped, that is."

"Then he might have known the move that killed Evan, right?" Nina asked excitedly.

"Yeah, but he's a bouncer. Most of them know a lot of moves like that. It doesn't make him our killer. What *is* suspicious is the fact that he hasn't been back to his apartment. We did some checking and nobody's seen him since Thursday afternoon. Greer was killed Thursday night. We'll lay low for a little while and if it looks like he's not going to show at all, we'll search his place and see what we come up with."

"Anything else?"

"You were right to think you knew him. He worked at Meyer Studios a couple of years ago as a security guard."

Nina thought back. Wes Timmins. Timmins . . . Yes, *now* she remembered. He'd been a little slimmer then and hadn't had the beard, but picturing Buck without it and wearing a guard's uniform, the memory came back. She'd recognized his voice because she always said good morning to him and he acted as if it was a great effort to mumble a greeting in return. He'd been surly then and not a particular favorite of anyone in the studio. "Did you learn anything more about him?"

"Details are kind of fuzzy, but somebody at TTS made a stink and got him canned. He had some trouble getting a job after that and hit the personal bodyguard and bouncer circuits. He's been brought up on a couple of charges of assault. One involved a woman." Nina drew in a sharp breath. "You okay?"

"Yes. I just . . . well, I just hope he doesn't know where I live. If he worked at the studio, he could have had access to our addresses."

"Already taken care of. I've got some boys watching your building. After I left last night, you were as safe as if you'd still been in my arms . . . maybe safer."

Nina wondered if Dino knew she was blushing. "What about the woman, Rose?"

"Tougher row to hoe. We can't seem to find anybody who knows her last name. Hell, Rose might not be her real *first* name. They could be hiding out together."

"Meaning, they might have something to hide?" Nina asked hopefully. "Enough to help Horst?"

"We don't know, Nina. All I can say is we're working on it. That bar you saw them coming out of seems like a good starting point. We're asking questions, seeing if anybody knew either of them, where they lived, etcetera. We already ran a comb over Greer's apartment. So far we haven't turned up anything, but we really don't know what we're looking for. Listen, I gotta go. And forget what I said last night about . . . things. Maybe we shouldn't analyze things too much and just go with the flow."

Nina hesitated. She didn't want to back off from the topic now that she and Dino had both gotten it out into the open, but this wasn't the time to belabor it. "I owe you a dinner," she said, dropping the other subject. "All we had last night was dessert."

116

"Deal. I just don't know when I'll be able to collect. I'll be in touch. Be careful. You did your bit last night. Let me take it from here, okay?"

"Yes, Lieutenant," she said, feigning the "obedient woman" routine.

"Good girl. Bye." Nina sighed as she hung up the phone. She had a strong hunch that Dino hadn't realized she was faking submission. She also sensed he was anxious over revealing some of his feelings about their relationship—he was a better doer than a talker. Physical expression came much easier for him than heart-to-heart talks. But they had at least scratched the surface of something that deeply bothered both of them, and she wasn't going to let it rest.

Nina was about to get dressed when she was buzzed by the day doorman. She went to the intercom and pressed the button.

"Yes, Jimmy?"

"There's a Ms. Dolan to see you."

"Send her up, Jimmy." Nina was intrigued. She hadn't spoken to Angela since she left yesterday afternoon. There had been no messages on her machine when she got home last night, and she found that odd. Robin usually called her just to say hi, but Nina hadn't heard from her after she had explained the results of Thursday night over lunch. Nina imagined Robin was embroiled in something time-consuming with Rafe . . . or Tom Bell. *He* had been at Jule's the night Evan was killed, too. Nina quickly dismissed any suspicious thoughts about Tom, despite his reluctance to join them at Jule's.

She thought about last night's conversation with Jay and his concern for Angela. For some reason, the brooch popped into her mind, and she made a mental note to ask Angela if she'd told Dennis that Nina now had it.

The doorbell rang, and Nina, still in her robe, answered it, to find Angela dressed as simply as she'd ever seen her. They exchanged greetings and Nina took her coat. Under it, Angela was wearing a cashmere sweater, tweed slacks and beige flats. She carried a newspaper under her arm.

"I'm sorry to just drop in," Angela said in a loud voice, taking in Nina's attire. "I'm not *disturbing* anything—or anyone—am I?"

"No, Angela. How's Horst?"

"Dreadful. He just left my place about an hour ago," Angela declared. "He's terribly worried about how bad things look for him with the police, of course, but he's also concerned about our beloved Helen, knowing she'd cut off her right arm if it generated bad press. He's very nervous— and with good reason. The smut is already stinking up some front pages!"

Angela tossed the paper across the room in Nina's direction. She caught it and unfolded the gossip tabloid to the first page. Among other lurid headlines, Nina saw the one that concerned Angela and Horst—"Daytime Diva in Deadly Triangle"—over a publicity still of Angela, looking jadedly glamorous.

"It's that bitch, Louise Davenport!" Angela stormed. "No-count southern trash is all she is. I've gone head to head with her before over the garbage she writes in that dirty dishrag her employer has the gall to call a newspaper!"

"Didn't you sue her or the paper once?" Nina recalled.

"Yes. And I won. I suppose this is her vindictiveness showing through the thin disguise of her so-called beacon-of-truth reporting."

"Is there anything here that isn't—er—accurate?" Nina asked delicately.

"No," Angela admitted regretfully. "It's just the way the facts are assembled. My phone has been ringing off the hook. Reporters have been dogging my footsteps. It's disgusting! I refuse to talk to the press. I've actually thought of taking a hotel room or something for a few days."

"That might not be a bad idea," Nina said, thinking of Jay's warning. She explained Jay's concern for Angela, whose eyes widened in fright.

"Then I was right," she said, paling.

"Right about what?"

"After I went to the police station yesterday, I went home with Horst. He eventually came to my place—he wanted to see if he could remember anything else by just being there."

"Did he?"

"No. But my babies were *anxious* when I got home, as if someone had been there again. I put it down to all the activity that has been going on. Later, when I was getting ready for bed, it seemed that things were just a little off in my bureau drawers and on my vanity. I'm very exact in placing certain items, but I've been in such a stressful state, I couldn't be sure that I hadn't been the one who'd moved things around. Now I think somebody *was* going through my belongings. But what in God's name could they be looking for?"

"I don't know. Maybe Evan was in possession of something the killer wanted, or they knew he had something he wanted to hide. Your place would have been perfect to conceal something like that."

Angela shook her head. "If we go on your theory that Evan was afraid someone might follow him to my house or wait for him there, why bring . . . whatever with him?"

"I see your point," Nina said. "Dino called and told me the police have been all over Evan's apartment. They didn't come up with anything."

"Maybe they don't know what to look for," Angela mused. She withdrew her Gucci key case from her purse, methodically going through the keys until she separated one from the rest. "Maybe we don't, either, but I have a key to Evan's duplex. I think *we* should take a look."

"Angela," Nina warned, "no!"

"I don't know why you're taking this attitude. I'd imagined you'd be the first to jump at the chance, knowing your inclination for this sort of thing."

Nina said, "First of all, Angela, I haven't told you what happened to me last night. Do you remember a security guard named Wes Timmins at the studio? He was fired a couple of years ago."

"Of course I remember him! I was the one who had him dismissed. I discovered he was sneaking into offices and dressing rooms and selling phone numbers and personal belongings on the black market to a fan club. He was an *odious* man!"

"He's also the bouncer at Jule's," Nina said.

Angela's eyes widened. "The one with the beard? Of course! I should have recognized his crude manner. He'd certainly have it in for me . . . and what better way to get revenge than to murder somebody in my own home!"

"If Timmins *did* murder Evan, I think he probably had a stronger motive," Nina said dryly. "But he knew about the fight with Horst, and he's also been missing since the night of the murder. He wasn't on the door at Jule's last night."

"How do you know?" Angela asked suspiciously.

"I was there. I also ran into him, almost literally, a few blocks from here. He was with Rose—she's the blonde we saw with Evan. When he saw me coming down the street, he came after me. Fortunately, I got away."

"So," Angela accused with narrowing eyes, "you've already been sniffing about, am I correct?"

"Yes, I have," Nina admitted, "but . . . "

"No *buts*, Nina darling! A man was murdered in my home, and someone I realize I care about very much is almost certain to be accused of the crime. We

120

both know that's a distinct possibility, and because of my thoughtless actions, I could be brought up on charges as well. Now it appears someone is violating my privacy, looking for God knows what. If *you* can play Dick Tracy, so can I!"

"I told you about last night so you'd understand the risk, the danger involved. Evan was not murdered in a very sophisticated manner. It was violent. I don't think either of us should subject ourselves to the same possibility."

"I don't care what you say, Nina, I'm going to go to Evan's place and see what I can find. As a friend and someone who has a certain amount of experience in these matters, I would think you'd want to help. Help me. Help Horst. And if, as you claim, Evan planted that card on his person as a clue for you, I'd think you'd want to respect his last wishes. *And* I think you know me well enough by now to realize I'll go through with this, with or without your help."

Nina spent the next ten minutes trying to dissuade Angela, but to no avail. Angela was ready to storm out, when Nina finally gave in. She'd do it, but not until after dark. She'd meet Angela there at seven. Angela, in rare burst of emotion, hugged Nina tightly, wrote down Evan's address, and left.

Nina decided to call Dino and ask him to come with them. But before she made it to the phone, it rang.

"Hello?"

"Nina, it's Dino."

"I was just about to call you. Angela and I . . . "

Dino didn't let her finish. "We found Rose. Her real name is Irene Rosen."

"Did you have a chance to question her?" Nina asked eagerly.

"No, and we never will. She's dead."

Chapter Nine

The rest of the day sped by much too quickly for Nina's liking. After she hung up with Dino, she tried to contact Angela to cancel tonight's plans, but she couldn't locate her. Horst was also unreachable. When Dino called Nina again later with more details on Rose's death, Nina decided not to mention anything about her and Angela's rendezvous, sure she would be able to head Angela off before it was too late.

Irene Rosen lived in Chelsea, on the ninth floor of a renovated building. She had been found, however, lying in a back alley with a broken neck. Some kids had discovered her body while retrieving a basketball.

In her apartment, the police found several pieces of expensive jewelry and a couple of gift cards signed in Evan's script.

The door to the terrace was open.

There were self-defense books on her bookshelf and an open bottle of vodka as well as several containers of pills on a coffee table. At the moment,

Irene Rosen was listed in police records as a possible leaper—a suicide. Everything fit. To Nina, it seemed to fit too well.

Irene Rosen might very well have been drinking and popping pills when someone came to her door. That same someone could have pushed her off the terrace. If she'd intended to kill herself, why didn't Rose take the easy way out by overdosing on drugs and booze? Why take a header?

No, there was more to it than that, and Nina was sure that Timmins was involved. There was still no sign of him, according to Dino. Dino was keeping his suspicions about Rose's death, if he had any, to himself. As he put it, he was "following up on a few things." Nina knew there would be the routine questioning of everyone in the building to find out if anyone had seen or heard anything out of the ordinary. Nina also knew the scene wouldn't be gone over very thoroughly unless foul play was suspected. Nina suspected it, all right, and Wes Timmins was at the top of her list of possible perpetrators.

It was now past six. She had been unable to reach Angela, and had had no opportunity to tell Dino about the plan, either—he'd rung off too quickly, and though she called back, he'd already left. Nina's only choice was to go to Evan's and try to talk Angela out of going inside.

Nina dressed in slacks, a sweater, and running shoes, then threw on a short fur-lined jacket. She worked hard to convince herself that Evan Greer's duplex was the last place Timmins would want to show his face, but she didn't do a very good job.

Nina had the cabdriver leave her on Central Park West, a block around the corner from Evan's place on Eighty-ninth Street. She felt terribly vulnerable as the car drove away. The wind was strong here, with no buildings to diminish its force as it swept across the park. She glanced at the stone wall that separated the far sidewalk from the park itself, imagining all sorts of nasty things lurking on the other side, then resolutely turned her back on them and walked down the street toward Amsterdam Avenue. Although the Upper West Side had made great strides in upgrading the neighborhood, Amsterdam still lacked the luster to attract the crowds that flocked to Columbus Avenue, with its glittering shops and popular restaurants. Even some of the cross streets in this neighborhood had uninhabited brownstones, their windows boarded up like patches over gouged-out eyes. Nina passed one and shivered, choosing not to look at it too closely. She did look behind her, however, and saw a man in a dark trench coat and fedora standing on the corner. He casually lit a cigarette, then turned and looked at Nina. Nina couldn't make out his features. He waited a bit, then crossed the street and disappeared down the block.

Nina shivered and quickened her pace.

Two-thirds of the way down the block, she found Evan's brownstone. Thick, sinewy vines of dormant wisteria scaled the full height of the building and disappeared over the roof. There were no lights on in any of the windows. Nina cautiously went up the steps and hesitated before she rang the doorbell. If Angela were inside, she'd have turned on the lights, wouldn't she? Nina checked up and down the street to see if Angela was in sight. She wasn't.

Nina tried the door. It was open. Now what should she do? What if there was someone other than Angela inside? She couldn't just stand out here. She gingerly pushed the door open, paused, and then, sticking her head inside the dark hallway, tried to look around.

Suddenly, she was yanked inside by an unseen

124

hand and the door slammed shut behind her. Nina let out a yelp.

"Shut up, for heaven's sake!" Angela hissed.

"Angela?" Nina whispered hoarsely.

"Of course it's me. Honestly, Nina, don't you think you could have lingered on the steps a little longer and been even *more* conspicuous?"

"I didn't know you were in here!" Nina replied testily. "There were no lights on, and . . . "

"There aren't *supposed* to be any lights on! This is the house of a *dead man!*"

"How are we supposed to look around if we can't see?" Nina retorted.

"I have a flashlight. And I basically know my way around. Come on."

"I can't see a single thing!"

"Really, Nina, stop whining," Angela snapped. "I sincerely hope you're not like this around your detective."

"Angela, wait," Nina said, raising her voice. "We mustn't do this. Something's happened that you don't know about."

"What?"

Nina told her about Rose. She couldn't see Angela's reaction in the dark, but could tell by her breathing, or lack of it, that she was disturbed.

"Do you think *she* did it? Killed Evan, I mean?" Angela whispered.

"My instincts say no," Nina said.

"Then we should go through with this."

"No, Angela! If Rose didn't kill Evan, then whoever did is still out there."

"That's right, Nina. They're out *there* and we're in *here* . . . and we're wasting time! Let's start upstairs." Nina gave up and reluctantly followed Angela up the stairs and down a hallway to a room that was partially lit by streetlights whose beams pried their way through the slats in closed wooden

125

shutters. Nina made out bulky furniture—a large bed, a towering wardrobe, and a bureau. As Angela began opening drawers and playing her busy little flashlight over their contents, Nina became distracted by the sound of footsteps on the sidewalk. They were slow, not the tread of someone intent on any particular destination. She risked easing one of the shutters open just a crack, and looked down.

It was the man in the dark trench coat—or at least *a* man in a dark trench coat. He stopped in front of the neighboring brownstone to light another cigarette, but his casual glance seemed to take in everything about Evan's building. The brim of his hat shadowed his face. The man's searching gaze stopped, and Nina swore he was looking right at her. She jumped back so fast that she bumped into a table.

"Sssh!" Angela reprimanded from across the room. Nina quickly ran over and struggled to switch off her flashlight. "What is *wrong* with you?" Angela hissed.

"There's a man outside. I saw him up at the corner of Central Park West. I think he followed me. Douse the light!"

"You're being paranoid, darling. One would think you've never done this before. I don't know how you've survived this long!"

"By being careful! Now just stop a minute and listen!" Angela did as Nina asked, then scuttled over to the window. She was about to peek outside, but Nina pulled her back. "He was looking right at that window. I don't know if he saw me or not."

"So what if he did? Despite the publicity, I hardly think everyone in New York knows Evan had lived here, that he isn't living, period." Nina listened and finally heard footsteps moving down the street. She let out a sigh of relief. "Can we be serious now?" Angela asked.

"Well, have you found anything?" Nina asked defiantly.

"Just a datebook on his bureau, but there wasn't a single entry in it."

"Didn't he ever have appointments?"

"Yes, but he had a very sharp mind. He kept almost everything in his head. He never even wrote down my phone number—he memorized it on the spot the first time we met," Angela said. "I imagine anything to do with business would be at the club office."

"How many rooms are there up here, Angela?"

"Four. The bathroom's at the top of the stairs, then a sort of music room, a cavernous hall closet, and the bedroom."

"Do they all have windows?"

"The closet, naturally, doesn't, nor the music room; that's kind of a little parlor. The downstairs is basically just one big living room, and a combination kitchen and dining area, with an additional full bath. But we're not done in here yet."

"We can't both work with one flashlight," Nina said. "But I can go into the music room, shut the door, and turn on the light in there without anybody seeing me." Angela didn't reply—Nina realized it was because she was holding the small flashlight between her teeth in order to free both hands for her search. Nina left her and felt her way down the hall, counting off the doors.

She walked into a room and, making sure there were indeed no windows, shut the door behind her, fumbled for the light switch, and flipped it on. She winced at the sudden glare of light, squinting until her eyes adjusted.

The room was very modern. A huge white lacquer cabinet dominated one wall, housing sophisticated stereo equipment and an expansive collection of albums. A modular grouping in the center of the room offered a place to relax and listen to music. Free-standing shelf units stood against one wall, a desk artfully squeezed between them. Nina's eyes swept the shelves. They were filled with books, small pieces of abstract sculpture, a pipe collection, and some antique humidors. The desk was neat—a phone, answering machine, some writing paraphernalia. This room looked like the set for a play or television show. Everything seemed to be in perfect order, just waiting for someone to make an entrance and start reciting lines. But someone had actually lived here, and there were no signs of it. It appeared that Evan had lived a very orderly, sterile existence.

Nina checked through a few drawers in the desk and found neatly filed utility bills, a lease, canceled checks, stationery, and an address book. Nina flipped through the address book, finding scant entries: restaurant suppliers, linen companies, dry cleaners, other restaurants. What few other entries there were were all initials rather than full names. She flipped through just once more and a tiny shred of paper fluttered out.

Nina examined it. It appeared to have been torn from the same book, possibly part of an entire page that had been removed. Nina sat down and carefully went through the book again. When she got to the B's, she noticed there was a jump in the alphabetical order. The list of names went from "Babcock Supply" to "Burroughs Lighting"—that left out a lot of vowels, and a few consonants, that could conceivably follow the letter B. Nina knew the police had searched here, but surely they wouldn't have torn out one page. Then who had? Evan himself? Had Rose had a key, like Angela? Timmins might have had one, or he might have broken in—so could a lot of people.

Nina spread the address book flat on the table and stared at Evan's phone. There was no blinking light to indicate that he had received any messages—the police had probably checked that out already. She picked up the receiver, and noticed the automatic redial button.

What if she pushed it? She might reach the last party Evan called on this phone. It might not mean anything. Then again, it might. What would Nina say to whoever answered? She tentatively punched the button and held the receiver close to her ear. Nothing happened for a moment. Then she heard a series of clicks, like the sound a rotary phone makes after you dial a number. Silence.

Then the phone rang. Once, twice, three times. Just Nina's luck—apparently no one was home. But just before she hung up, the ringing stopped and an answering machine picked up the call. A man's mellifluous voice came on the line, identified himself and the number, and politely asked whoever was calling to leave a message at the sound of the tone. There was a pause, then a beep, and Nina quickly hung up in shock.

The voice had identified itself as belonging to Tom Bell.

Nina tried very hard not to jump to any conclusions, even though Tom had been at Jule's the night Evan was murdered. And "Be" certainly fell between "Bab" and "Bur". . . .

The lights in the room suddenly went out. Nina felt her heart go into overdrive.

"Nina? Nina?" It was Angela. Nina swiveled in the chair as Angela entered the room, whispering in alarm.

"What's wrong?"

"I shut off the lights in here. I think there's someone else in the house!"

"Are you sure?" Nina asked, hoping against hope that Angela was wrong.

"Yes. Don't move. I heard a noise, like someone bumping into a chair on the first floor."

"Didn't you lock the door when we came in?"

"I don't know. I was so concerned with getting you in and getting up here, I don't remember."

Great, thought Nina. *Now* what did they do?

"*Now* what do we do?" Angela said, echoing Nina's thoughts aloud.

"We try to get out," Nina whispered.

"How?" Nina sensed Angela close by. She reached out a hand in the dark and brushed against Angela's arm. Angela gasped. "It's me," Nina whispered. "The first thing we have to do is be calm. Next, we listen. If there's someone here, they'll probably check the bottom floor before they come up here. The stairs are close to the front door. We make sure whoever's downstairs is in the back of the house, then we run like hell out into the street."

"Why can't we just stay here?" Angela whimpered.

"Because there's no place to hide in here, and only one way out. Come on." Nina took Angela's hand and pulled. She tugged harder, and Angela reluctantly followed Nina carefully across the dark room. As far as Nina remembered, there were no obstacles in their path between the desk and the door. It seemed like hours before Nina's fingertips felt the cool, hard surface of the wall. If she was correct, the door was inches to their left. As quietly as she could, she eased the door open a crack and listened. She heard nothing. They waited.

Nina eased back inside, shut the door, and in a low voice said, "I don't hear anything. It's possible whoever came in heard *us*. Maybe they were just as concerned about being seen as we are and they left."

"What if they didn't?" Angela quavered.

"Do you want to stay in this room all night?" Nina asked irritably.

"No. . . ."

"All right. Then we make our move. Keep your ears open. Is there a back door?"

"Yes—why?"

"I just like to have options, that's all," Nina replied.

The two women crept out, holding their breath. There were no sounds from downstairs. A pale glow filtered up the stairway from the streetlamps that shone through the first-floor windows. It would give them enough light to get down the steps without breaking their legs or their necks.

They crept. They paused. They listened, then crept again. Nina counted off the steps. They were almost there—Nina could see the front door. But just as Nina's forward foot touched the foyer floor, she saw a shadowy figure looming in the living room entry. She barely had a chance to gasp as the stranger silently blocked their escape.

Angela had seen him, too, and Nina heard her let out a small squawk of dismay as she stumbled down the last two steps. Everything else happened very quickly. The figure reached out and the hall lights came on. Nina caught a glimpse of a dark trench coat and hat. The man grabbed Angela's arm and pulled her around the balustrade to make a run for the back door, but another figure barred their way.

The only emotions Nina had time to feel were combined relief and humiliation as she recognized the second man. It was Dino. And he didn't look happy.

Chapter Ten

Nina spent a great deal of Sunday in a foul mood. Not even Chessy's concerned attention could snap her out of her irritable state of mind. Damn Dino!

As it turned out, the man in the trench coat was a cop—Dino had detailed him to keep an eye on Nina after her run-in with Timmins, to make sure nothing happened to her. He had followed her to Evan's house, then called Dino. Rossi decided to teach her—and Angela—a lesson.

Even Nina's assertion that she had originally wanted Dino to be involved in their nosing around didn't placate him. Stone-faced, he forced Angela to turn over the key and tore into both of them for their irresponsible, foolhardy behavior. Angela lapsed into silent indignation. Nina fumed.

Dino had his man drive Angela home, while he escorted Nina personally. Neither said a word. Nina knew if she opened her mouth, she would be cut off and subjected to Dino's standard steely tirade of warnings: Be his eyes and ears when he asked, sit home and be a good little girl when he didn't. She was, after all, just a civilian. And a woman.

Dino stopped the car in front of Primrose Towers so abruptly that Nina thought her neck might snap.

"Sorry," he managed to say between clenched teeth.

Nina bit her tongue to keep from reminding Dino that he had promised never to say that word to her again. She realized it would be petty and childish. Since she couldn't think of anything else to say, she said nothing. She unbuckled her safety belt and let it spring back with a loud slap. Dino was staring straight ahead, drumming his fingers on the steering wheel.

Nina extricated herself from the car with as much dignity as she could, shut the door gently but firmly, and without offering so much as a "good night," marched with her head held high toward the lobby, where she paused for a split second, hoping for some reaction from Dino. She wanted to hear his door slam, wanted to hear his voice tell her to wait, wanted him to at least ask if she had come up with anything as a result of her efforts. Instead, she heard him gun the engine and torture his tires as he peeled out.

Fine! she thought, as she rode up in the elevator. He'd thrown down a gauntlet, so she'd rise to the challenge. Dino would be in a bad mood for a while. He'd be silent. From now on, he'd keep this case to himself, letting Nina in on none of the details or developments. But that didn't mean she'd sit quietly by and twiddle her thumbs!

There was nothing in the Sunday paper about Rose. Nina didn't know if that was good or bad. She supposed no one had been able to reach her next of kin yet, so the information was being held back. It looked as if Horst was getting into safer waters. If the police could prove the blonde had committed suicide, it meant they had their murderer. If they couldn't, the killer was still on the loose. And they couldn't possibly suspect Horst of killing Rose—he'd been with Angela that night.

The new wrinkle concerning Tom Bell disturbed her. Nina called Robin several times during the day but always got the machine. Then she tried Rafe, and got his. She wanted to talk to Angela but wasn't sure exactly what kind of mood she'd be in, so she decided to let Angela call her. Angela didn't. But then, neither did Dino.

Nina was very glad when Monday morning finally came, and she could clear her head for a while by immersing herself in her work. She'd had all day Sunday to memorize her script and had attacked Tuesday's as well.

Nina's new story line was already beginning to take shape. Melanie Prescott was footing the bill to bring some mysterious power broker into town. She was trying to court him away from his corporate throne to set up residence in mythical Kingston Falls for a while. Morgan Fowler, as the new character was named, didn't seem to have a background Melanie could dig up too much dirt about. Obviously, he was the man who was going to throw the costume ball that Robin had mentioned—the event to which Nina would first wear the wedding gown . . . and the brooch.

Earlier on Monday morning, Nina had recovered the brooch from her purse and tucked it away in her shoulder bag. Now as she walked through the doors of Meyer Studios, she could almost feel its presence, as if it were a live thing, suffocating in the confined space and struggling to get out. Nina would be very glad to turn it over to Dennis or Jason. And if these

134

weird feelings about it persisted, she'd simply insist on wearing something else, foolish or not.

Nina was early. There was no one in the rehearsal hall, but the coffee maker was full and a platter of sticky Danish was in readiness. She poured herself a cup of caffeine and headed for the dressing rooms. As she turned the corner, she saw Tom Bell lingering in front of her door. He turned with a broad grin.

"Hi," he said cheerfully. All his anxiety of the last several weeks seemed to be gone. "I just knocked on your door—I thought Robin might be in there talking with you."

"No," Nina replied. "I just got in. Is the door locked?"

"I don't know. I didn't check. I guess it's too early for Robin to be in though, huh?"

"Yes, I guess it is." Nina thought he was looking a little nervous around the edges.

"How was your weekend?" he asked.

"Oh, the usual," Nina managed to say with a straight face. Actually, for her it had been—the same old thing. Murder, breaking and entering, a fight with Dino. Yes, the usual.

"Looks like coffee's ready," he said. "Think I'll go get some. See you at rehearsal later." Nina watched Tom move down the hall. He glanced over his shoulder once, gave a little wave, and disappeared around the corner. Was Nina reading more into this than necessary, or had it been odd that Tom didn't ask how Angela was or mention anything about Horst? And what was Tom's connection with Evan? *Was* he connected to Evan's death?

Nina tried her door. It was indeed locked. She opened it, flipped on the lights, and began her morning routine, but it was soon interrupted by Horst. He didn't look any more rested than he had on Friday.

"Morning, Nina," he said with a weary smile.

"How are you?" Nina asked, rising and going to him.

"Okay, everything considered. Angela told me what the two of you did on Saturday. She's written out today, but on behalf of both of us, thanks."

"You're welcome," Nina said. "Try not to worry. I know that's easy to say, but I'm sure it'll work out."

"You didn't hear, did you?" Horst sighed.

"What?" asked Nina, afraid of the answer.

"The police questioned me again. Angela, too."

"When?"

"Yesterday afternoon. They wanted to know where we were on Friday night. We gave each other an alibi—I don't know if they believed us or not."

"Why were they questioning you about Friday night?"

"That girl who was killed, Irene or Rose."

Nina clenched her teeth. "Who questioned you? Was it Lieutenant Rossi?"

"No. As a matter of fact, Angela hit the roof and asked that Rossi be brought in. They said he was no longer on the case."

"What?" Nina gasped.

"You haven't heard from him?"

"No. We didn't part on very good terms on Saturday night," Nina said. "Horst, please don't worry about this. I know you're innocent. . . ."

"Until proven guilty," Horst said, almost to himself. "I wonder how many people think I am?"

"No one who really knows you," Nina assured him.

"The police don't know me. The D.A.'s office doesn't know me. Neither does the press. Not good odds. But Angela's been wonderful through this. We've both learned a lot about ourselves and each other. We're closer than we've ever been. I guess that's something. I did chew her out for going to Greer's apartment. It could have turned out a lot differently. I know *you* have an instinct about this kind of stuff—you've certainly proven that—but Angela doesn't. I don't want to see her hurt on my account, or you, either."

Nina smiled slightly. "I think Angela has turned in her badge."

"And you?" Horst asked.

"That's between me and the wallpaper." They exchanged a long, silent look, then Horst nodded, said he'd see her later, and left, passing Robin on the way out.

"Got all your calls yesterday," Robin said brightly. "Rafe and I decided to breathe a little clean air and went to visit the folks upstate. They've got a great country house outside of Rhinebeck. It felt good to walk on ground instead of concrete for a while. It's even colder up there, but the house has a wonderful fieldstone fireplace. It made warming up twice as much fun."

Well, Nina thought, Robin certainly seems to be in a good mood.

"I didn't want to say anything in front of Horst," Robin went on, "but has there been any good news?"

"I wish I could say there was. Not to change the subject, but does all this sweetness and light mean that things are simply swell with you and Rafe again?"

Robin beamed. "Yeah. It was all my fault, really. You know that Rafe originally came to New York to pursue a career in theater. Well, between TTS and me, there just wasn't enough time for him to do that. Rafe is so damned attentive, I started feeling guilty, thinking I was keeping him from his dreams. I didn't want him to look at me one day and say, 'If only . . .' I thought if we cooled things down for a while, he'd go for it, but his seeing that play the other night changed his thinking. The pull isn't strong enough for him anymore, at least not to make him want to do theater full time. He's happy here, for now, but he'd like to do some films and other TV shows. And most of all, he wants me to be a part of it. He even wants me to appear with him in summer stock—star houses, you know." She took a deep breath. "It was a big risk for me to take! I could have lost him. But he loves me, Nina, more than anything. He loves me even more for giving him the space to find himself."

"I understand," Nina replied. "It was very unselfish of you. It's called 'loving with open arms.' It's not easy to do, and I'm proud of you. But . . ."

"What?"

"I know this is a very blunt question, but it's important. During the time you gave Rafe his . . . freedom, did anything happen between you and Tom Bell?"

Robin looked as if she'd been doused with a pail of cold water. "Nina, how could you ever *ask* such a thing? I'd *never* be unfaithful to Rafe, not if there was the slightest hope he'd come back to me."

Nina had already put her foot in her mouth. She decided to go all the way up to the knee. "Several people have seen you and Tom together in rather—intimate moments. You've both been acting—well, odd lately, and after we all saw Tom at Jule's the other night and he wouldn't join us . . ."

"Please don't ask me any more about Tom," Robin said firmly, drawing into herself. "I can't talk about it. I made a promise to Tom, and it could do him a lot of damage if certain things he told me got out."

"Then you're protecting him?" Nina asked carefully.

"Sort of."

Nina wanted to press, but she couldn't, not without admitting that she thought Tom might be involved in the murder of Evan Greer. Still, she feared for Robin's safety if Tom actually *was* involved.

How could she go about this delicately, but effectively? Nina didn't get the chance.

"I really have to run, doll. I want to go over some lines with Rafe before rehearsal. Let's forget you asked me about Tom, okay? I know you've been under a strain recently with Dino, and now this thing with Angela and Horst. See you later." Robin walked out, leaving a distinct trail of frost in the air.

Nina frowned. What was going on, anyway? Why had Dino been taken off the case? And why hadn't he called to tell her about it? Well, if his macho pride wouldn't let him get in touch with her, she'd call *him* at lunch.

Nina decided to pick up her costume for the day and get the brooch back to Jason or Dennis, whoever wanted it. She left her dressing room and made her way to the costume department, passing a few cameramen and audio technicians she knew. She smiled and greeted them warmly, but her mind was elsewhere. What if someday she discovered that someone she'd worked closely with for years had actually committed a crime? What if that person was Tom Bell?

Before she knew it, she had almost reached Jason's office. The official wardrobe room where fittings were made, costumes pressed, and accessories kept was farther down the corridor. Here, and lining several other hallways, were big metal lockers, each containing the articles of clothing the actors wore. Most had wide strips of masking tape plastered on the outside with the characters' names scrawled in Magic Marker.

Now Nina heard arguing—two men. It sounded like Jason and Dennis, but she'd never known either of them to raise their voice, especially not to each other. She was about to clear her throat or bang against a costume locker to let them know somebody was coming—until she heard Evan Greer's name.

Nina tiptoed along the hall until she was right outside Jason's door.

"Keep your voice down," Jason warned.

"But they think Krueger killed Evan," Dennis said.

"Do you want everything to come out, Dennis? Is that what you want? I helped you with Greer, and . . ."

"I didn't ask for your help, damn it!" Dennis wailed.

Nina heard a scuffle, then a crash as something fell over near the door. She positioned herself to move away quickly if necessary.

"It's over, Dennis. Greer's dead, and the world's a better place. So far it looks like the police have no idea that I was the one who kept phoning Greer at the club that night. They'd have been pounding on my door already if they had. Just lie low and wait for it to blow over—for both our sakes. Nobody can prove anything."

Nina had heard enough. She backed away from the door, turned, and ran as quietly as she could down the hall, glad that the carpeting softened the noise of her tread. Her head was spinning.

First Tom Bell, now Dennis and Jason! All thoughts of returning the brooch vanished as Nina quickly made her way back to her dressing room and shut the door behind her. She thought about the page missing in Evan's address book. There were so many names that could have been written there—Bell, Buck . . . or Jason Barnes. Actually, there was another one. Jay Benedict, the bartender. But it would have been perfectly logical for Evan to have Jay's number on that page. Buck's, too, for that matter. Tom Bell and Jason Barnes were another matter entirely.

Somehow the hard studying that Nina had done on her lines the previous day was for naught. She kept making mistakes all the way through rehearsal.

Nina managed to fudge her way through everything until lunch break finally arrived, when Horst and Spence Sprague took her aside and asked if she was all right. Nina apologized for her lack of concentration and promised she'd be fine when it came time for taping. She only hoped she would be!

When she returned to her dressing room her costume for the day was hanging on the rack. Good—she wouldn't have to face Jason until she took her outfit back to wardrobe at the end of the day. What did she know about Jason? He'd come to TTS a year or so after Nina. She remembered hearing that he'd gone through a very rough period after a divorce. Lately he'd been seeing Renee Reynolds, the musical director. She made a mental note to talk to Renee later and see what she could find out.

There was a knock on the door.

"Yes?" Nina asked.

"It's Horst." Nina opened the door and was surprised to see Jay with him. Nina was at a loss for words.

"What . . .?" she began.

"I was in the neighborhood," Jay said, making the phrase sound every bit as trite as it was.

"And I was on my way out to meet Angela for lunch," Horst told Nina. "I heard the page say you had a visitor, so I went out front and saw this young man. I told him I thought you were still here and I'd deliver him to you in person."

"If it's a bad time, Ms. McFall, I'll understand," Jay said nervously.

"No, no—come in, please," Nina said, gesturing for him to enter.

"I'll see you after lunch, Nina. And don't forget to brush up on that last scene."

After Horst had left, Jay said, "I *have* come at a bad time, haven't I?"

"No, it's just that I'm a little distracted today."

141

"How's Ms. Dolan?"

"She's not here today. But she and Horst Krueger, the man who just showed you in, are going through a very difficult time. Mr. Krueger is the chief suspect in the murder of Evan Greer."

"What?" Jay looked very surprised.

"Don't you read the papers?" Nina asked.

"I didn't see anything the day after Greer was murdered," Jay said.

"It took a while to get out. And you probably don't know about the woman called Rose, either."

"What about her?" Jay asked.

"She's dead," Nina said flatly. "Looks like suicide."

Jay grew very somber and sat down on Nina's divan. "I guess I shouldn't be surprised. If you ask me, she was a manic depressive—scary mood changes. You never knew what she was really thinking or what she might be capable of. . . ."

"Couldn't Evan see that? I mean, maybe she could have gotten help or something."

"She didn't want help. Didn't think she needed it. And people who are that far gone . . . well, there's either no helping them at all and they rot in a padded cell somewhere, or they put on such a convincing act that they get out again. Once you've gone over an edge, nothing can bring you back—*nothing*. And sometimes it drives the people you care about right over the edge with you." He stopped, obviously thinking he was rambling too much, and looked at Nina. "I think maybe we should change the subject," he said, forcing a smile.

"I do, too. I assume you came here to take me up on my offer."

"Maybe. I just want to see what it's all about."

"Well," Nina said, "the casting director is here today. She'll want to read you."

Jay looked puzzled. "What does that mean?"

"Do a cold reading of a scene. Like this." Nina handed him some pages from the day's script that involved Melanie. "Why don't we give it a try?"

"Right now?"

"Why not? I've been having some trouble with that scene you've got, and I need to go over it. We'd be doing each other a favor. Go ahead. Just read. Don't worry about making mistakes—even pros trip over a word now and then."

Jay glanced at the script for a moment, then began. Within two lines, Nina was involved in the scene. Jay was, too. His reading wasn't polished by any means, but he was damn good for a beginner. When the scene was over, he looked self-conscious again.

"Go ahead—tell me how bad that was," he mumbled.

"It wasn't bad, Jay. Actually, it was pretty good."

"You're kidding!"

"No, I wouldn't do that. I don't believe in encouraging someone who I feel has no talent. I think you do. But you'd have to develop it."

Jay's face lit up. "Thanks, Miss McFall! I've never really had too many ambitious goals or anything. I guess I'm not like other people."

Nina smiled. "I don't know you well enough to say if that's true or not. But from what little I *do* know, I think you're being wasted at Jule's."

Again, as it had on the first time Nina met Jay, an elusive shadow passed across his face. "I serve a purpose there. I have a job. I do it well. Dom's been very good to me. I don't want to let him down."

"You mean by leaving?" Nina asked.

"Yeah. . . ."

"I know you're not a native New Yorker—I can tell by your speech. Where did you grow up?"

"Outside of Boston," Jay responded. "I lived with my aunt, came here about five years ago. You really think I can do this?" he asked eagerly.

"Yes, I do. You'd have to enroll in some acting

143

classes, but I'm sure we could get you some extra work here, so you can feel your way around, get some expertise by watching from the sidelines."

"You know what else I'd like to do? If it's not too much trouble," Jay added hastily.

"What?"

"See everything. Take a tour, like a fan or a tourist or something."

His boyish enthusiasm touched Nina, and she smiled.

"I think that could be arranged, too."

"Great!" Jay said with a huge grin. "I can't tell you how much this means to me!"

Nina took Jay up to meet Olivia Smith, the *Turning Seasons'* casting director, knowing that Olivia never went out to lunch until quite late. The minute Jay walked in the door, Olivia's eyes lit up. Nina explained the situation to Olivia, asking her to read Jay as a favor and then arrange for someone to take him on a tour of the studio when he was done.

Nina left Olivia's office feeling better than she had all day. Since she was right down the hall from Renee Reynolds's office, she decided to stop in for a little chat.

Renee was an elegantly slender, dark-haired woman in her mid-thirties, and she had an engaging laugh that always brightened Nina's spirits. Renee was always up, her blue eyes sparkling. She usually had a good word or a positive thought for the day. And she knew her job. The incidental music that underscored TTS's scenes was always right on the money. She had an inexhaustible knowledge of current hits, movie themes, and old standards. She also worked with unknown musicians and songwriters and occasionally used their melodies on the show.

Nina found Renee at her desk, sorting through a pile of cassettes. She was dressed casually in designer jeans and a silk blouse. Silver bracelets tinkled on her wrists.

144

"Hello, Renee. Got a minute?" Nina said.

"Sure, Nina. For you, anything. Haven't seen you in a while. I hear Jason made quite an impression on you with that wedding dress."

"That he did," Nina assured. "He's quite an amazing man."

"Isn't he!" Renee said with a warm smile. "He's just full of surprises."

"How long have you two been seeing each other?" Nina asked.

"Two years and counting."

"That sounds serious," Nina said, sitting down on a chair in front of Renee's desk.

"Yes, but we're still cautious. We're both creative people, subject to the usual moods, artistic tantrums. We both need solitude, space, sometimes. And we both have tempers."

"I can't imagine either of you blowing up," Nina said, smiling.

"Believe it! Jason more so than I. There's no talking to him when he's ticked off. I just give him room and he goes out with the boys and blows off some steam." Renee paused. "Sometimes he blows off too much."

"What do you mean?" Nina asked.

"I've had to bail him out of jail a couple of times," Renee admitted.

Nina's eyes widened. "Really? For what?"

"I don't know if it's because of his job or what, but Jason sometimes feels the need to assert his masculinity. When he take me out on the town, we don't go to chic restaurants and cocktail lounges. That's fine— I don't like them either, but sometimes we go to real dives. And every once in a while, if a guy lays it on a little heavy with me, Jason gets his back up. Then his fists go up too, and the guy goes down. When he was in the navy, he was an amateur boxer. He tells me he likes to keep in practice." Renee laughed. "Boys will be boys, I guess."

145

A boxer. Nina didn't like that at all.

"Was there something special you came to see me about or are you just schmoozing?" Renee asked now.

"A little of both," Nina said. "Actually, there *is* something you might be able to help me with. I—uh—I got this note on one of my fan letters," she went on, thinking on her feet. "It's written like a poem, but I wondered if it was from a song or something."

"Do you have it with you?"

"No, but I think I remember some of it. 'Ah! May the red rose live alway To smile upon earth and sky!' Then there's something about the beautiful weeping or dying. . . ."

"Cheerful message," Renee commented. "Actually, it *does* sound familiar, but I can't place it. I'll look into it, if you want."

"I'd appreciate it, Renee. No rush," Nina added, lying. "It's driving me crazy because I thought I knew it, too. You know how it is when something gets in your head. . . ."

"Indeed I do. Consider it done."

As Nina walked numbly back to her dressing room, she felt as if she'd betrayed Renee, pumping her for information about Jason. What the hell was she doing, prying into the lives of other people all the time, looking for dark secrets and motives? Nice lady you are, Nina McFall!

When Nina returned from grabbing a quick bite of lunch, she was told there was a call for her. She went to the phone at the front desk, and was surprised and delighted to hear Dino's voice. He sounded tense.

"Nina, I need your help," he said. "I'll pick you up at your apartment around seven-thirty, okay? Please say yes."

How could she possibly say anything else?

Chapter Eleven

That evening at ten minutes to eight, Nina was seated at a table at Jule's opposite Dino. He'd been very quiet when he picked her up. She knew there was a lot going on under the surface, but she waited patiently. She was sure Dino had plenty to say—he'd say it in due time. There was a light crowd, not many of them having dinner, so Dino and Nina were flanked by empty tables.

Nina occupied herself by smoothing out some wrinkles in the skirt of her cream-colored linen suit. The weather had changed radically, a warm spell moving in degree by degree. Then she arranged her purse on the table to her left. She took a sip of water, admiring the single rose in the Victorian vase. Roses—so many roses in this case. . . .

"I took myself off the case," Dino said abruptly.

Nina snapped to attention.

"I had to. I was getting a lot of flack from the D.A.'s office—they didn't think I could handle it objectively because of my previous involvements with *The Turning Seasons*. . . . and with you."

"Me!" Nina said. "The *D.A.* knows about us?"

"Word gets around, Nina. Ever since Krueger was first brought in, I've been pushing to keep the case open, looking for other avenues. Some people thought I was wasting the department's time and the taxpayers' money. I got fed up when I learned they were bringing in Ms. Dolan and Krueger to question them about Irene Rosen's death, so I bowed out. Unofficially, however, I'm still poking around. They've set me up with another case already, but that doesn't mean I can't dig around on the side. I've got friends who will pass me things on the sly. One of them is a readout from the phone company listing all calls made from Evan Greer's office over the past few months. I recognized the number of Meyer Studios. Greer called there frequently."

"That's logical," Nina said. "Angela apparently received a lot of calls from Evan."

"I took that into consideration, but a couple of things don't add up. There are calls dating back to *before* Angela was seeing Greer. I'd like to know who he was contacting." Dino pulled out a computer printout from his jacket pocket. "If you can, look this over. Since Greer was in his office at night more often than not, I'd like to know if he called anybody in the TTS cast or crew at home."

Nina had a sinking feeling that she knew who might have received some of those calls. "I have a contact sheet at home, for mailing Christmas cards and such. I'll go over them tonight," she promised.

"Thanks. I'd call the studio myself, but I have to cool it."

"I understand. What about Rose?"

"Her neck was broken, but the M.E. seems to think there's a possibility the break wasn't caused by the fall." Nina noticed that Dino was avoiding looking her straight in the eye. He wasn't allowing any personal subtext to get in the way of their professional discussion.

"And Timmins?" Nina asked.

Dino frowned.

"It's like he vanished off the face of the earth. Makes him look guilty as hell. But if he planned to skip town after bumping Greer off, why wait? Why hang around and go after Rose the night you saw him?"

"If he killed Evan, maybe he thought Rose knew something. Maybe he killed her, too."

"I'm certainly not axing him from the suspect list. We searched his apartment and found enough drugs to open a pharmacy. Some of the stuff matched the pills in Rose's apartment. Even if he's innocent of murder, he's going to be sent up for a while—*if* we catch him."

"Maybe Greer knew about that," Nina said. "Evan seemed to be the type of operator who liked to keep his hands clean. If Timmins was supplying drugs to some of Evan's associates, Evan may have wanted to put a stop to it."

Dino said nothing, but he was looking into her eyes for the first time that evening.

"You've got a sharp mind, lady," he finally said. "Too bad it's surrounded by a headstrong brain. I'm still ticked off at you, in case you're wondering. Not so much at the fact that you went to Greer's place, but because you let Angela talk you into it. You may have a lucky star over your head, but I don't think she does. I'm *responsible* for you, damn it, and everybody you drag along. Remember that conversation we had the other night, about going out with somebody who's always at risk? The shoe fits the other foot, too. I've got as much to lose as you do. Yet you get all bent out of shape because I'm in danger, then turn around and put yourself in danger as well. A little hypocritical, isn't it?"

His words stung. "Yes, Dino, I guess it is," Nina said meekly.

"I respect you, babe. You're not like the other women I've known. Yeah, I have pretty traditional ideas about how men and women should act. I can't help that or change it. It's the way I was brought up. Hell, maybe if you *were* conventional, I wouldn't be so crazy in love with you. And all that adds up to making you a rare and precious gift. I don't want to exchange it. I don't want to have it stolen. And I sure as hell don't want to lose it!"

"Stop it, Dino, before you make me cry in public. That's what you want, isn't it?" Nina said tenderly. "You want to see me do something typically foolish and feminine, don't you?"

Dino smiled, reached across the table and took her hand. "You're very good at both sometimes," he replied, his eyes twinkling.

Nina playfully slapped his hand and composed herself. How could she possibly stay mad at him? She couldn't. "Why did you bring me here?" she asked.

"Well, you've hung out at pizza parlors with me and Pete, and we've had dinner at some of the joints I like, so I thought I'd take a stab at entertaining you in the manner to which you've grown accustomed. Besides, I kind of like this place. Clientele's a little superficial, but I can concentrate on the decorations— and you. Besides, you never know what little pieces of info you can pick up when somebody realizes you're off duty." He looked around. "What do you have to do to get a waiter? I noticed you didn't have any trouble the other night—you had a waiter *and* a bartender at your disposal."

"I know the owner," Nina replied smugly. "If you hadn't come the other night, I would have been dining with him."

"Oh, yeah? Dinner's fine, but don't push it. Besides, I've already spoiled you for any other Italians."

Nina laughed and glanced around the dining area. More people were coming in now. The bar was crowded. She saw Dominic there, ordering a drink. He turned, spied Nina, and smiled.

"Speak of the devil," Dino muttered.

Startoni started moving toward them. Nina noticed he seemed in a very mellow frame of mind. And he'd obviously been drinking heavily again. His steps were a little unsure.

"Nina! We meet again. And Detective Rossi, we also meet again!" Nina and Dino exchanged a glance. "I guess it's safe to assume that you're together? No, don't answer—none of my business. Romance is a very private thing. Its joys and mysteries are not for prying eyes. I remember it well. . . ." Dominic stared off into space for a minute, teetering precariously on the balls of his feet. Nina wondered if he was thinking of his wife, and felt a stab of pity for him. She also hoped he wouldn't fall.

"Would you care to join us?" Nina asked.

"No, but thanks," he said. Then he turned to Dino. "Jay told me about Miss Rosen. Another tragedy. Another death. It doesn't seem to balance out. It's like a war—men and women dying for reasons they don't really understand, all for some selfish higher power's greater good. And you, Mr. Rossi," Dominic continued, his eyes a little glazed, "you pick up the casualties and try to arrest the guilty. I don't envy you. I wouldn't have the detachment to deal with the innocents who get caught in the middle. I liked Evan," he rambled on. "Aside from whatever he may have done, there was some goodness in him. Trust me. There was, I know. And obviously there is a lot of good in *you*, Nina. I heard what you did for Jay today. I'm very happy. He needs to get away from this place, to have a life of his own. It's time he cut a few strings from his past. He's been tangled up in them too long. . . ."

"Dom, are you okay?" Jay said, suddenly appearing beside Startoni.

"Jay. We were just talking about you. You're gonna be a big television star and leave us all behind!"

Dino looked very confused. Jay put a gentle hand on Dominic's shoulder, but Dominic shook it off, almost roughly.

"I'm okay, Mr. Benedict," he said, spitting out the name as if it were a dirty word.

"Have you had dinner?" Jay asked.

"No," Dominic replied. "Guess I should, shouldn't I?" Suddenly his manner was quiet, almost apologetic.

"Yes, Dom. I'll send something up."

"Want to join me?" Dominic asked.

"I can't leave the bar, Dom," Jay said, looking nervous.

"All right. Dinner for one. I'm gonna have to do something about that. Soon. Soon, right, Jay?"

Jay's face clouded. Nina could see that his patience was wearing thin, but it was also clear he cared for the older man. "Come on, Dom," Jay persisted.

"Stop calling me that," Dominic snapped. "You want a business relationship with me, you call me Mr. Startoni or you don't call me at all! *Capisce*?"

"Yes, sir," Jay replied, color flushing his cheeks.

"Okay, okay." Dom turned back to Nina and Dino. "Pleasure. Enjoy yourselves. You're very lucky, both of you. *Buona notte*." Dominic meandered off. Jay looked torn between going after him and staying at Nina and Dino's table.

"If you want to go . . ." Nina began.

"No, that's okay. I hope he didn't bother you. He gets that way sometimes."

"It's his wife, isn't it?" Nina asked.

Jay hesitated a second, then nodded. "Thanks for the PR job and the tour."

"Did Olivia think she could use you?" Nina asked.

"Yeah. I'm supposed to call her tomorrow and set something up. Like I said, I can't thank you enough. Let me get you a waiter." Jay moved off, and Dino scowled at Nina.

"I didn't follow any of that," he said.

Nina quickly explained, then she talked a little about Dominic and the void in his life caused by the loss of his wife. Dino nodded, lost in some private thought. Silently, he reached under the table and put his hand on her knee.

"Startoni was right," he finally said. "We *are* lucky."

The waiter came and they ordered. While Dino was asking what kind of beer Jule's served, Nina decided to check her makeup. She reached into her purse and pulled out her little makeup mirror. Immediately she noticed it had several scratches on it.

"What's wrong?" Dino asked. "You're looking into that thing like you're seeing somebody else."

"I don't understand. Something's scratched the glass, but that's impossible. There's nothing in here that could do that."

"When did you use it last?" Dino asked absently.

"I had it in my purse when I came here with Angela. There was nothing in it then that would do this, either."

"Keys?"

"No, they were in the pocket of my coat. The only other thing in here was . . . " Nina suddenly remembered. "That brooch!"

"The one Angela handed you?"

"Yes, but that couldn't have scratched it. It's just a piece of costume jewelry that one of the prop men picked up for twenty dollars. The stones are too big to be real. They'd be worth a fortune if they were. Do you know anything about jewelry?"

"I know diamonds can cut glass," Dino said. "Rubies, too."

She still hadn't returned the brooch. She'd taken it home with her today—Jason hadn't been in wardrobe or his office when Nina brought back her costume this afternoon, and she hadn't wanted to face Dennis after the conversation she'd overheard.

She flashed back to the nightmare she had in her dressing room. The brooch had haunted the corners of her mind wherever she went since the first time she'd seen it.

"You just may have stumbled onto something," Dino said thoughtfully.

Nina thought she might have, too. Diamonds were supposed to be a girl's best friend. But what were rubies?

Chapter Twelve

After Dino had dropped Nina off at Primrose Towers, she dug out her contact sheet and sat down to cross-reference the numbers Evan had called from his office at Jule's with the home phones of the TTS family. It was almost too easy.

But it wasn't without its surprises.

The moment Nina arrived at the studio the following morning, she sensed something was wrong. Helen was flying around even more like a harpy than usual.

In the rehearsal hall, several members of the cast were milling around. Nina spied Horst and went over to him.

"What's going on?" Nina asked.

"The studio was broken into last night," he said grimly.

Nina's green eyes widened. "Really?"

"Well, not exactly broken into," Horst amended. "It seems someone didn't do a very careful job of checking things last night. One of the windows in the men's room wasn't shut all the way. Looks like that's how whoever it was got in."

"Was anything taken?"

"That's the strange part. Jason noticed some things tossed around in the wardrobe department. Some of the office files were pried open and a couple of dressing rooms showed signs of forced entry, including yours. But nothing was taken."

"That doesn't make sense!" Nina said.

"That's not the weird part. Some cast members found money slipped under their dressing room doors this morning."

"If I didn't know any better," Nina said, "I'd swear you were making this up! Somebody sneaks into the studio, doesn't take anything, and *leaves* money?"

"You got me," Horst sighed. "Naturally, Helen's furious. She's firing security people left and right. Her first concern, of course, was the long-term story lines. They were in her office, but nobody hit there."

"I guess the police have already been here."

"Been and gone. Not a print anyplace."

Just what we need—another mystery, Nina thought. Then she realized that "Buck" Timmins knew the layout of the studio. But why would he take the risk? And what connection could there be between wardrobe, dressing rooms, and the main office files?

"I've got to get to my office," Horst told Nina.

"Is Angela here?"

"Yes, we came in together."

"Good. I need to talk to her."

Horst left the rehearsal hall as Tom Bell came in. The moment he saw Nina, he turned and left. On impulse, Nina decided to follow him.

She was on her way toward the dressing room area when Olivia, followed by several extras for today's show, came down the stairs from the upper-level offices and stopped her. Several of the extras stared at

Nina with big smiles of recognition and whispered among themselves.

"Just taking the troops down to check in with the stage manager," Olivia explained. "I wanted to let you know how impressed I was with that young man you brought to my office yesterday. I want to try him out—with Helen's permission, of course—with a few lines. Maybe a bartender or something, to make him feel at home."

"What a good idea," Nina murmured, frustrated that she'd lost Tom.

"I wanted to use him today," Olivia went on, "but there's a new rule that you have to show proof of U.S. citizenship—passport or birth certificate or something— before you can get a job doing *anything* these days. Jay said it might take a while for him to come up with it, but he promised to call me today and let me know."

Olivia ushered the extras off like a flock of young chickens under her motherly wing. Nina continued her search for Tom.

She had just reached the dressing room when a door opened and Angela flew out in a huff. She saw Nina and exploded.

"Look at this!" she said, voice dripping with disdain. She shook a black wig under Nina's nose. "Do you *believe* this? They want me to wear *this* at that ludicrous costume ball. Never!"

"Angela, calm down." Nina knew Angela was under a lot of tension and was using the wig as an excuse to blow off steam.

"I have perfectly good hair, darling. I certainly don't intend to hide it under this— this *thing*! And in case you haven't heard, I'm involved in your new story line. We're going to be fighting over the same man. Ridiculous!"

"How do you know?" Nina asked.

"I demanded that Helen tell me or I'd walk off the

set. *Gothic!* Really, how passé That sort of thing went out with *Dark Shadows.* And to top it all off, *you* win the man! But it's anything but a bed of roses, darling, let me tell you. You remind this Morgan Fowler person of his dead wife, and he traps you in a bedroom with that silly wedding dress, and . . . "

"Angela, *please.* I don't have time for this. But I do want to ask you something. I need the name of a good jeweler. I want to have something appraised."

"What?" Angela asked, curiosity immediately replacing her outrage.

Nina checked the hall to see if they were alone and withdrew the brooch from her handbag. "This."

"Why? It's fake."

"I don't think so, Angela. I think it might be worth a lot more than anyone first imagined. But please keep this to yourself."

"I will—*if* I can go with you. The man I have in mind is an odd sort. Actually, some people think he's a fence. He might be suspicious of you if I'm not there."

Nina didn't know if she believed Angela, or if Angela was using her story as an excuse to tag along. "All right," she said reluctantly. "I'd like to go at lunch."

"Fine. Now if you'll excuse me, I have to talk to Helen." Angela started off down the hall, then turned. "And you should check your dressing room. Mine was broken into. Nothing was taken, but then again, the charitable crook didn't leave me any money, either. Maybe *you'll* be luckier!"

My dressing room can wait, Nina thought. She went instead to Tom Bell's door and knocked. There was no answer.

Frustrated, she decided to make Jason Barnes her next stop. There had to be a rational explanation for his and Dennis's involvement with Evan Greer. But they obviously had something damaging to hide, and she didn't want to expose their secrets to Dino and the police unless it was absolutely necessary.

Jason wasn't in his office, but she found him in wardrobe. He and several of his assistants were taking inventory, double checking to make sure nothing had been stolen or damaged.

"Hello, everyone," Nina said. Damn! She'd hoped to catch Jason alone. There was a round of greetings, then everyone went back to their work. Nina went over to Jason. "I heard what happened," she said.

"Nina, the brooch. Do you or Angela have it?" he asked immediately.

"I do," she said. Jason sighed in relief. "Angela gave it to me the night Evan Greer was killed. I've been meaning to return it to you or Dennis or at least tell you that I had it, but I've been terribly busy. I was surprised that one or both of you hadn't called Angela or me in a panic."

"I've had a lot on my mind lately, that's all, what with the costume ball coming up," he said. "Why don't you just keep the brooch with you? Obviously it's in safer hands than it would be here."

"Was anything damaged?" Nina asked.

"No, thank God." Jason delicately picked up the wedding dress he'd designed. "I was scared to death when I saw this on the floor. I don't know who was in here, but if I ever find out, I'll break their neck!" Nina shuddered, knowing he very well might. "I have a big favor to ask you, Nina," Jason went on. "I know this may be putting you out, but would you mind keeping this dress at home? At least for a few days until things calm down a little?"

"Of course, if you'll trust me with it," Nina said, surprised.

"I do. I think you know what it means to me."

What an odd combination of personalities he was, Nina thought. An ex-boxer with, in one corner, a lace wedding gown, in the other, a brutally battered opponent. A wise guy in a bar with a fat lip. A dead man in Angela's parlor. . . .

"I'd like to talk to you later, in private, when you have a minute," Nina said.

Jason looked at her suspiciously. "What about?"

"It's . . . personal."

"Okay, Nina. I'll try, but I got my hands full here. How about lunchtime?"

"I'll be out then, but I'll come back at the end of the day. Maybe things will be more settled by then." Jason nodded. "Oh, by the way," Nina added, trying to sound casual, "is Dennis in yet?"

"No. He called in sick—said he'd try to come in later. Prop department's a mess, too. You'd think whoever did this would have been a little less obvious about it. Somebody must have been desperate to find something or just wanted to mess things up. I'll put the dress in a garment bag and leave it in your room later, okay, doll?"

"Sure. But I *do* need to have that talk with you. I'll see you later." Jason went back to work and Nina went back to her dressing room. She certainly wasn't getting very far.

Rehearsal was very uneven, punctuated by Helen's occasional outbursts, Angela still ranting about the wig, and Horst's obvious nervousness. Robin and Tom were unusually edgy. Again, Nina noticed whispered exchanges between them. It was fortunate, she decided, that Rafe wasn't on the show that day. Though Nina tried, she couldn't get Tom alone. He and Robin were the first ones out the door when lunch was called. Nina was about to follow them when Angela appeared, ready to go to her jeweler.

His first name was Bernie—Nina never caught his last name. His shop was on Forty-seventh Street, near Sixth Avenue, on the second floor of a building

160

right smack in the middle of the diamond district. Here, between Fifth and Sixth Avenues, Forty-seventh Street was nothing but watch and jewelry stores.

Bernie was a jolly little man in his sixties with a bald head and wide eyes. His white shirt, a tad too small for his well-fed belly, was wrinkled, the sleeves rolled up to his elbows, and he wore the brightest orange tie Nina had ever seen. He beamed at both Angela and Nina.

"Miss Dolan, how nice! You brighten my day more than my diamonds do. And you have a beautiful friend. How nice. Special occasion? Birthday, anniversary, engagement rings? But of course, no—there would be handsome gentlemen on your arms if that were the case. What is it I can do for you?"

"Bernie, this is Nina McFall," Angela said.

"I know who she is. I have my little television in the back. I always watch *The Turning Seasons*, ever since you first came in, Miss Dolan. And you are both lovelier in person."

"Thank you," Nina said.

"Nina would like something appraised, so I brought her to the best man in town."

"That's right, you did!" Bernie said, jiggling with laughter. "Miss McFall . . . Nina. A nice name. A derivative of Ann, from the Hebrew—'full of grace, mercy and prayer.' So. What is it that you've brought me?"

Nina took out the brooch and handed it to him. "I'd like to know if this is worth anything."

"Ahh," Bernie said under his breath. "You came by this in inheritance, or what?"

"Actually, I—I found it in a secondhand store, but I had it in my purse and it scratched a small makeup mirror."

"The brooch did that? Hmmm." Bernie held the jewelry up to the light, then took out his eyepiece and focused in on it. "So. So. Interesting setting. Dramatic choice of stones. You are right, Nina. These stones did indeed scratch your mirror. Any of them could have done it—the onyx, the diamonds, or the rubies."

Nina and Angela stared at each other in amazement. "But—but it only cost twenty dollars!" Nina gasped.

"Then the person who sold it to you is a fool. It is old, very old. You've been carrying around a small fortune—maybe more than that."

"What do you mean?" Nina asked, puzzled.

"I do not want to say now. I have to make some calls to some old friends in the business. So. May I hold onto it?"

"Well . . . " Nina began.

"I can understand your caution. But if this is what I believe it to be, I will not want to keep it any longer than I have to—and neither will you. I say no more. Come back, please, later this afternoon. It will be waiting for you. Good-bye."

Bernie wandered into his back room, muttering, and Angela and Nina walked numbly out of the shop. For once, neither had a single word to say.

Chapter Thirteen

Nina and Angela arrived back at the studio before the lunch break was over. Nina didn't know what was running through Angela's mind, but her own thoughts were jumping like a three-ring circus. She hadn't made any headway with what she'd discovered on the phone record; she still had three suspects among the *Turning Seasons* cast and crew. Buck was still at large, and now she had a possibly priceless brooch— priceless and something more by the way Bernie had acted. Funny, just not having it in her possession seemed to lift a great weight off her shoulders. How could something like that wind up in a secondhand shop? She kept remembering Bernie's words: "I will not want to keep it any longer than I have to—and neither will you." Maybe it was cursed? No, Nina decided; that crazy thought must have surfaced because of the new story line. It fit in, somehow—antique wedding gown, a man mistaking Melanie for his dead wife, a cursed brooch. But it was the stuff of fiction, not reality. And Nina's reality right now was trying to help Dino solve a murder. Maybe two.

Nina and Angela parted by the rehearsal hall, Angela saying she'd go with Nina to see Bernie later. Nina considered looking up Tom Bell, but imagined he and Robin were still out lunching—or whatever. So she decided she'd go onto the set, maybe run through her blocking once or twice. This was going to be an easy week on the show. She was written out tomorrow and Thursday, but she had to be there Thursday afternoon when they read actors for the part of Morgan Fowler, Melanie's bizarre new love interest.

She found Spence Sprague in a quiet corner with Merrill Vaughn, the set designer, going over some floor plans. Merrill reminded Nina of a college dean, all pomp and bluster. His face was noble looking, all severe angles. His large, owlish eyes observed the world from behind very thick glasses. Those eyes, combined with his balding head fringed by white hair around the ears, commanded a certain respect. He always wore tweeds, no matter the season, and they diffused the aromatic scent of tobacco wherever he went.

"Hi," Nina said, as she strolled over to them. "Scenic pow-wow?"

"Nina," Merrill said crisply. "I'm glad you're here. I'd like you to see this. It's a rough draft of the setting for your new story line."

Nina gazed at a ground plan and some sketched elevations. Here and there were dabs of paint, indicating the proposed color schemes. It was the foyer of a mansion, a sweeping spiral staircase dominating center stage. Huge Palladian windows lined a small landing where the stairway split in two, steps going off in opposite directions. The other sketches showed a bedroom, drawing room, and huge dining hall.

"It's gorgeous," Nina said. "It looks like a haunted house!"

"Precisely what I intended," Merrill responded.

Obviously he took Nina's comment as a compliment, but as usual his features betrayed no emotion.

"Is this house supposed to be in our little town?" Nina asked.

"Yes," said Spence. "On the outskirts. *Way* on the outskirts. It's the place you help find for this Fowler character. He refurbishes the old house, turning it into a Victorian showcase."

Nina immediately thought of Jule's.

"Everyone in the scenic department is very excited about it," Merrill said. "In fact, everyone I've talked to is. It's going to be something entirely different. Just what we need around here. I've grown quite lethargic, coming up with new plans for endless tasteful restaurants and sterile office space. *This* is going to be fun!"

Merrill returned his attention to Spence and his sketches, and Nina wandered over to the set of her "sterile office space." She was halfway through miming her scene when Renee came in.

"Thought I might find you here," she said. "Don't you ever stop striving for perfection?"

"Never," Nina replied. "One day I might even achieve it!"

"I've got info for you on that poem. I've been trying to unearth some old-fashioned parlor music for this Gothic thing. Last night I was listening to some vintage records that I got from the library, and suddenly I heard the very words you recited to me coming out over the stereo."

"You're kidding!" Nina exclaimed.

"The song is called, appropriately enough, 'Ah! May the Red Rose Live Alway.' It's by Stephen Foster. He wrote it in 1850. A lot of people think he wrote only minstrel-show songs, but the style of this song was closer to his heart. I can make a tape of it for you, if you like."

"Oh, I would, very much. It sounds fascinating."

165

"It is," Renee said. "I listened to the song a couple of times and found myself humming it when I came to work this morning—that and "Beautiful Dreamer," also by the illustrious Mr. Foster. Jason's hooked, too."

Nina concealed her start of surprise. "Jason was with you when you were listening to the song?"

"Sure. It's kind of fun. We both sit and listen to the music, see how it makes us feel. If it evokes the right response for *both* of us, I know I'm onto something. Jason's a sentimentalist at heart."

"Did you tell him I asked you about the lyrics?"

"Yes, why?" Renee asked.

"Just curious. I saw Jason this morning and he didn't mention it," Nina said, hoping she sounded nonchalant.

"Jason's got a lot on his mind this morning. Actually, he's been a little out of it for a few days. He won't talk about it, so I don't push. The macho image won't let a woman help, you know."

"Do I ever," Nina sighed. "Well, thanks again."

"No problem. I'll get that tape to you. See you around."

After Renee left, Nina sat down at Melanie's desk. "Ah! May the Rose Live Alway." An old song. Evan's bouquet. Black roses . . . Something was tickling the back of her mind. Little pieces of the puzzle that had been missing were suddenly in view. They didn't fit together yet, but Nina knew if she jiggled them around enough, they'd settle into a picture.

When she looked up from her desk, Tom Bell was staring at her. They were alone on the set.

"I want you to leave Robin alone," he said without preamble. His tone was so weary that it didn't come across as an order. "It's between her and me, okay? I know how you are—tell you not to open a box and you will the second everyone's back is turned. Don't bother. There's nothing pretty inside this one."

166

His shoulders slumped, and he turned away.

Nina had to say it. "How did you meet Evan Greer?"

Tom's entire body went rigid and he whirled to face her. "How did you know?" he asked, his face white.

"It doesn't matter . . . unless you were involved in his murder," Nina said softly.

Tom moved so quickly toward Nina that she instinctively drew back. He leaned over, holding onto the desk for support. "I didn't kill him. I just have rotten timing and rotten luck," he muttered.

"What does that mean, exactly?" Nina asked.

Tom sighed. Then the words tumbled out in a flood.

"All right. Robin asked me to tell you this when you started asking her questions—I didn't want anybody to know, but she said you'd understand. I've got a disease, Nina. It's called gambling. I like the ponies. I like good odds. But they've both been against me for a long time. If you know anything about Evan Greer, you know he had a hand in everything. He could help you place a bet on anything from horse racing to cockfights. A buddy of mine from the track turned me on to him. But I got in way over my head. I owed a lot of people a lot of serious money. My bank account was wiped out, if you can believe it. I was deep in a hole.

"Evan felt sorry for me," Tom continued, "He was an odd guy—he'd help you get a fix on your vice, but go easy on you if it busted you. The other people I owed money to weren't so generous. I was threatened. Evan gave me some tips. Only problem was, I didn't have any cash. So I started stealing. I was stealing petty cash from the dressing rooms right here in the studio. Robin caught me. I told her the truth. She promised not to say anything if I returned all the money. I swore I would when I got back on my feet. And I *was* getting there. But I had to pay back the rough numbers first. I was almost in the black again. The only person I still owed was Evan. Twenty grand. He called me Thursday afternoon, but I wasn't around. I went to the club that night. Evan told me it was no sweat—he had some deal going, the cash I owed him didn't matter. Boy, was I relieved! Then I bumped into Robin. She hadn't known about Evan, so I had to tell her. When Evan was killed, my debt died with him. It could have looked real bad for me. I was sweating it out. Robin believed I was innocent and never said a word. She's a good person and a good friend. I don't consider myself much of either."

"Then the money that 'appeared' under dressing room doors this morning came from *you*?" Nina said.

"Yes. I swore I'd pay everyone back, and I did. Thing was, I picked a rotten time to do a good deed. Everyone around here seems to tie the money in to the break-in. I *didn't* do that." He hung his head. "Now you know it all. It's the truth."

"I believe you," Nina said, and she did. "Don't worry. I won't say anything."

"Thanks, Nina. Robin was right about you." Without another word, Tom straightened up and left the set. Nina compassionately watched him go. Tom's home phone number was not on the list that Dino had given her.

One down and two to go.

The cast started drifting in for the final run-through. Horst and Angela were together, Angela still bitching about the wig. Then Angela's mood suddenly changed, and she clutched Horst's arm. Nina followed Angela's gaze and heard a general commotion.

Standing in the door was Sergeant Charley Harper with a uniformed officer and a plainclothesman Nina had never seen before. He walked up to Horst and Angela.

"Lieutenant O'Connor, NYPD. Are you Horst Krueger?"

"Yes," Horst said, wincing as Angela's fingers dug into his arm.

"I'm here to arrest you for the murder of Evan Greer."

Chapter Fourteen

Helen Meyer reacted to Horst's arrest with her typical "show first, me first" attitude, showing no regard for the pain of her individual drones. She pulled every string at her disposal, finally managing to stave off his incarceration until Tuesday's show was in the can.

Angela's lawyer arrived at the studio before the final run-through. The cast and crew were very supportive of Horst, who looked worse than Nina had ever seen him. But that was only natural. As soon as the words "It's a wrap" were out of the stage manager's mouth, Horst was led away.

Nina's heart was heavy as she took off her make-up. She'd tried to get in touch with Dino, praying there was something he could do despite the fact that he wasn't officially on the case, but he wasn't around. She removed her costume and dressed mechanically. How could this have happened? She tried to talk to Charley, who would only tell her, on the Qt, that Irene Rosen's death was now considered a suicide, and not to quote him. It looked as if Rose had been written off as a grieving lover, not a remorseful murderess.

Hanging up her dressing robe, Nina noticed a heavy garment bag on the clothes rack. Jason had obviously come in while she was taping and left the wedding dress for her to take home. There was a note pinned to the outside in Jason's block printing that said simply, "Thanks."

Angela burst in, wearing her street clothes and carrying the black wig. "I'm going to the police station," she announced. She saw the garment bag. "Are you taking something home?"

"Yes. . . ."

"Good," Angela said tersely. She unzipped the bag and threw the wig into it. "*Lose* this, darling. If enough of them disappear, they'll get the message. I'll call you." She started out.

"Angela, if there's anything I can do . . ."

"There's nothing to do. I'll move heaven and earth to stop this travesty. Just watch me!" Holding her head high, Angela stalked out of the room with a regal gait—a queen on a mission to prevent the beheading of her beloved consort.

By the time Nina was ready to leave, the studio was almost empty. She decided it was time to talk to Jason and Dennis. Carrying the dress over her arm, she went to wardrobe, only to be told by one of Jason's assistants that he'd left for the day. Nina then went to props. Dennis hadn't come in that day at all.

Nina hated the implications.

Remembering her appointment with Bernie, she took a cab to his shop. He wasn't around, either. Instead, a younger, more fastidious version of the owner manned the counter. He introduced himself as Bernie's son, Jacob. Nina explained why she was there.

"Yes, Ms. McFall," he said, nodding his head. "Pop watches your show all the time. He left you a message. He'd like to meet with you someplace—maybe private?"

"All right," Nina agreed. "Do you know what he found out?"

"Pop was tight-lipped. Never seen him like that." He shrugged.

Nina gave Jacob her home address and phone number, saying that his father could drop by later that evening whenever it was convenient—she would be home all night.

She hurried home, hoping to find a message from Dino. Carefully hanging the wedding dress in her closet, she checked her answering machine. There were only two calls: one hang-up and the other from Robin, who wanted to thank Nina for believing Tom and not passing judgment on him.

Nina was very restless. She fixed a hasty meal of broiled chicken, most of which she couldn't eat, so she cut up the remains and gave them to a grateful Chessy. Pouring a glass of chilled Chablis, she sat down at the dining table to go over the computer printouts of Evan's calls again, starting with the night he had died and working her way backward. She ignored the studio and cast-member numbers—Tom Bell's home phone was not on the list and neither was Jason's. The only one on the contact sheet that matched the printouts was Dennis Dale's.

Willy buzzed Nina from the lobby to say that there was a Mr. Bernie Cohen to see her. Nina asked Willy to send him right up. Maybe hearing about the brooch would take her mind off Evan and Horst for a little while.

Bernie arrived seconds later, wearing a wrinkled tan raincoat over the same outfit he had worn earlier. Only his manner had changed. Gone was the "how-nice-to-meet-you" attitude, replaced by something very serious, almost grim.

"Thank you for meeting me," he said somberly.

"Can I get you something? Wine? Coffee?" Nina asked, ushering him into the living room.

"No, thank you. I will say what I have come to say, then, please, forget I was ever here." He nervously removed a piece of black velvet cloth from his coat pocket and placed it gingerly on the table. Turning back the corners, he revealed the brooch. It might have been Nina's imagination, or just the fact that she hadn't looked at the brooch for a while, but it seemed to glow with a malevolent light.

"Rubies," Bernie said. "Do you know anything about them?" Nina shook her head. "To this day," he continued, staring at the brooch, "Burma still provides us with the finest and largest supply of these stones. The Burmese held them as sacred stones, guarding the mines as if they were religious temples. Do you know what they said about these stones?"

"No," Nina said softly. She found herself mesmerized by Bernie's voice as if he were an ancient storyteller.

"They believed the gems carried the spark of life, which could heal the sick in mind and body. They were a good-luck charm and even more. If a ruby was implanted beneath the skin of a warrior, he would be invisible."

Nina raised her brows. "But what about *these* rubies? You gave Angela and me the impression there was something mysterious about them."

"There is—if you believe."

"Believe what?" Nina asked.

Bernie paused, collecting his thoughts. "In 1886, when Burma became part of the British Empire, the natives lost their monopoly on the ruby mines. There was hostility on both sides. One of the heads of the English mining company on Burmese soil was a man named Arthur Borden. As the story goes, being an adventurous sort, he would occasionally work in the mines himself. Supposedly, he discovered one of the largest stones ever unearthed—a hundred thirteen carats."

Nina's eyes widened. "My goodness!"

"Some of them have been found even larger," Bernie said. "Anyway, Borden's stone was the most admired color, the finest color, known as pigeon-blood red."

Nina recalled the blood the pin had drawn from her thumb and shuddered.

"Borden coveted the stone," Bernie said, "and had it smuggled back to England, so the story goes. But the ruby was flawed, a shadowy flaw called a 'cloud,' giving the ruby's center a very dark quality. Reluctantly, and also for the purpose of concealing the fact that he was in possession of such a large stone, he had it reduced to thirteen stones, each one weighing seven flawless carats, and turned them into a suite of jewelry for his wife, Rebecca. The entire collection was composed of a ring, a necklace, a stickpin, earrings, a bracelet—and a brooch."

Nina stared at the gleaming piece of jewelry. "Are you trying to tell me . . . ?"

"Yes, Miss McFall. To the best of my knowledge, this is a piece from that suite."

"But how on earth could something like this have wound up in a secondhand store in New York?"

"I haven't told you the rest of the story. The suite of jewels was always passed on to the firstborn daughter of the Borden family. Arthur's grandchildren moved to America and settled in Boston, where they became one of the richest, most powerful families of their time. Many of them believed it was because of the rubies. Finally, the suite was passed on to Julia Borden, one of several 'black sheep' in the Borden clan. Rebellious and hopelessly romantic, she shunned the suitors her parents urged upon her and secretly fell in love with a dock worker from the Boston waterfront. To make a long story short, they ran off together. There was talk of a child. The family was beside themselves—and not only because they'd lost their darling Julia. When she left, she took the suite of rubies . . . are you still with me?"

"I think so," Nina said, though she was growing more skeptical by the minute. Yet, what would Bernie have to gain by telling her a story like this if it wasn't true?

"Let me remind you, Miss McFall, that this is a story, like many others, that enhances the notoriety and worth of old gems. If you do not believe it, you would not be the first. The rubies were not good luck for Julia, or her lover. She trusted him completely, but behind her back, desperate to make his mark in the world, he sold the pieces one by one to build a financial empire."

"And then?" Nina asked, caught up in the story almost against her will.

Bernie shrugged. "Then nothing. That's where the story ends. Some say Julia's lover tried to buy them back after he had amassed his fortune. Some say the family bought them back, paying enormous sums, or that others gave the pieces back readily, claiming they were cursed and had brought nothing but ruin. Other stories suggest that the family even killed to retrieve the stones. One murder happened right here in New York, about five years ago, although no one could connect it to the family. As far as I know, it's still an unsolved crime. I can imagine whoever had this brooch kept it for as long as they thought it was safe. Things that appear in the windows of secondhand stores have their histories. Not all of them are pleasant."

There was a long, silent pause. Then Nina cautiously reached out and took the brooch in her hand. The rubies lost some of their brilliance. "I've noticed," Nina said, "that at times the gems look— different."

"Different how?" Bernie asked.

"To use your word, clouded. It's like the fire dims inside."

"Not uncommon," Bernie stated. "It's part of the myth surrounding the stones—*if* you believe. When a ruby casts little light from within, as the tales go, it means great misfortune for the owner. And I wouldn't be surprised if these stones have a darker shadow than most, when you consider the name of the ruby, which is also the name of the suite of jewels."

"What is it?" Nina asked nervously.

"I did not tell you? So. Listen. Look at the setting— the onyx patterned like leaves, the diamonds that look like drops of dew. That was all intentional. It goes back to the original shadowy flaw in the uncut stone. Arthur Borden's ruby was called the Black Rose of Burma."

Chapter Fifteen

An hour later, Nina was driving downtown in her Mazda. She'd picked it up from the service station on Sunday but had had no real occasion to use it. Now she did. Driving always cleared her mind.

The Black Rose.

Bacharrat roses. Angela had told her they were sometimes called black roses. If Evan had meant to leave Nina a clue, he couldn't have given a more obvious one, and Nina had unwittingly been carrying it around with her ever since his death.

She reached out and felt the lump in her purse resting next to her on the front seat. Could the possession of this brooch really be the motive for Evan's killer? Though Nina still had trouble believing all of Bernie's story, he'd said the brooch was worth an incredible sum of money. That in itself was a motive. But what did the brooch have to do with Evan?

Nina thought again about the missing page in Evan's address book. "Black Rose" would have fit between the entries that still existed. But then again, so would "Borden." And "Buck." And "Barnes." Driving wasn't clearing her head at all. She realized she had to take care of something first before it drove her crazy. There was something she had to know, and the only person who could tell her was Dennis Dale.

She remembered his address from the contact sheet—she'd stared at it for a long time. Now as she drove down Seventh Avenue, she realized she wasn't very far away from where he lived. She entered the West Village and began checking street signs. From here to Chambers Street was probably Manhattan's most confusing area. There were no more numbered streets—they had names like those in a small town—MacDougal, Perry, Spring, Charles, Bank. Dennis lived on Perry Street, a quiet, tree-lined stretch of brownstones surrounded by the colorful madness of Greenwich Village.

Nina miraculously found a parking place and made her way down the block.

She found Dennis's building and went into the entranceway. He lived in apartment 3B. She pushed the buzzer and waited for a response. There was none. Maybe Dennis really had been ill today and had stayed home for a legitimate reason. He might be in bed. Still, Nina rang again and this time Dennis's voice came over the intercom.

"Who is it?"

"Nina McFall, Dennis. I hate to bother you, but it's important." The connection was cut. Nina was debating whether to ring again when a loud buzz sounded, indicating that Dennis was letting her in. She grabbed the door and opened it just before the buzzing stopped and started making her way up the three flights of stairs as she mentally went over what she was going to say to him.

By the time she reached the third-floor landing, she was out of breath and her knees were shaking.

Nina didn't know if it was the ascent or nerves. She could be walking straight into danger—but she kept telling herself there was no way that Dennis could have killed Evan *and* Rose. There had to be an explanation.

Nina rang the bell, and in a few moments Dennis answered. He was barefoot and dressed in faded jeans and a worn, navy T-shirt. He didn't look sick—just very nervous.

"Hi," he said weakly. "This is a surprise."

"I know, Dennis," Nina said. "I heard you were ill today. . . ."

"I'm much better now."

"Good." They looked at each other for several seconds. "You wanna come in?" Dennis said at last.

"If you don't mind. I realize it's rude of me to just drop by like this, but I do want to talk to you."

Dennis looked down at the floor and rubbed one bare foot over the other. "Sure, come on in."

Nina thanked him and entered. She heard him close and lock the door behind her. The apartment was small but tastefully done. All the walls were white, the furniture predominantly black with red and white accents. A black art deco vase occupied a half-moon table under a mirror. There were red roses in the vase. Nina shivered. Would she ever be able to look at a rose again and feel anything but revulsion?

"This is very nice, Dennis," she said with forced cheer.

"Thanks. It's kinda small, but it's just me here. There's a kitchen," he said, indicating a doorway closed off by white shutters, "and a bedroom and a bath. Actually, it's bigger than a lot of places down here."

Nina smiled and nodded.

"Can I take your coat? It gets pretty hot in here most of the time." Nina agreed and Dennis helped her take off her coat. He carefully hung it on a black

179

lacquered coat tree. His actions were very slow, as if he were stalling for time. "Haven't got much in the kitchen, but I could make you some tea or something."

"No, really, Dennis, I can't stay long." Where do I start? she asked herself. Dennis indicated that she should sit. She did, on the edge of the sofa. Dennis slid into a chair across from her and played with a loose thread on his shirt.

"So what can I do for you, Ms. McFall? None of the actors have ever come here—not that I expect them to. I guess we're all in the same ball club, just different strings." He pulled harder on the thread.

Nina looked him straight in the eye. 'Did you hear about Horst Krueger?'

Dennis nodded. "On the news. Bad luck."

"It's more than that, Dennis. Horst is innocent."

"Lots of people are," Dennis said softly. "It's no guarantee you get an even break."

"I'm trying to help him," Nina said.

"So, why come to me?" Dennis replied. Again they met each other's gaze. Dennis suddenly rose and turned his back to Nina. "No!" He shoved his hands in his back pockets.

"Dennis . . ." Nina began, but she never had time to finish the sentence. The white shuttered doors to the kitchen suddenly slid open, revealing Jason Barnes. Nina instinctively jumped to her feet.

"Don't worry, Nina," Jason said quietly. "Nobody's gonna hurt you."

"Jason, you—you said . . ." Dennis stammered.

"I know I told you to deny everything, Dennis, especially to Ms. McFall here, but I was wrong." Jason moved into the room. His size seemed to dwarf everything. "Sit down, Nina. Dennis is innocent. He didn't kill Evan Greer. But, yes, he knew him. I did, too. Dennis also knew Rose."

180

Nina sank back down onto the sofa in shock. She hadn't expected that.

"You heard us arguing in my office, didn't you, Nina?" Jason asked. Nina nodded. "Your perfume gave you away—I smelled it the minute I went out into the hall. I just didn't know how much you'd overheard. After Renee told me about the little talk the two of you had, and when you asked to speak to me in private, I knew. But I wanted to talk to Dennis first. He's wanted to come forward, but . . ."

"How did the two of you know Evan Greer?" Nina asked.

Jason looked at Dennis.

"Tell her," he quietly said to Jason. "Go ahead."

"You sure?" Jason asked, almost tenderly. Dennis nodded. Jason went to him and put a fatherly arm around the young man's shoulder. Dennis leaned against him for a minute, then, very embarrassed, quickly moved away.

"I met Greer through Dennis," Jason began. "About ten months ago, I'd had a pretty rough day and stopped in a bar on the way home from work. It was a ritzier kind of place than I usually like to go to, but I just wanted one for the road. There weren't many people in there. Pretty soon Dennis came up, ordered a drink and we started to talk." Jason stopped and stared at Dennis, obviously waiting for some sign from him either to stop the story or continue. Their eyes met, then Dennis looked at Nina.

"I was a hustler, Ms. McFall," Dennis said. "Men, women, it didn't matter." He looked at Nina, waiting for a response. When she didn't look shocked or disgusted, Dennis continued. "It just sort of happened to me. I didn't have any skills, any real education. A woman in a bar offered me money to go home with her once. The first time something like that happens you get high. This woman wanted me *that* bad. The second time it happens, you just see the money. The third time, it was Evan Greer. But he didn't have any intentions of following through. Turns out he just wanted to know if I'd do something like that. When I said yes, he said he'd take care of everything. He arranged 'dates' for me—friends of his from out of town who needed an escort. Rose was one of the others in Evan's stable, except she supplied some extras. I went out a lot, saw places and things I never would have otherwise. I went with men, women, people who just needed somebody to talk to. There was never any sex—Evan said that was too risky these days. You see, he took care of me that way."

"Yeah," Jason said in an angry rumble. "Regular Boy Scout!"

"I know how you felt about him, Jason," Dennis said, suddenly flaring, "but Evan *did* have a good side. Everything isn't all black or white!" Jason just shook his head. Dennis, getting very emotional, continued his story. "Anyway, like Jason said, I met him in this bar. Things had been slow with Evan. I needed some money. It took me quite a few drinks, but Jason was kind, gentle, almost like . . . like a father figure."

Nina chose not to say anything. There was ground here that Nina didn't think Dennis and Jason had ever really covered. She was only a listening bystander.

"Jason made it clear to me he had a girl and didn't need any favors. But instead of punching me out or walking away from me, he got me to talk. I was pretty confused emotionally by that point, and I really fell for Jason. He made me feel safe. And he made me feel like I was capable of more than what I was doing with my life. He got me the job at TTS and we became friends."

"But Evan wouldn't leave him alone," Jason cut in.

182

"Dennis had been real popular with some of Greer's friends, and he kept calling Dennis, harassing him to take a few jobs on the side. What was wrong with a little extra money?"

"One night," Dennis said, "I gave in. There was this older businesswoman from Chicago. I kinda liked her. We went to the opera. We ran into Jason and Renee. It didn't set too well with Jason, and we had a big argument. By this time, Jason knew all about Evan. He threatened to go after him. Evan let up for a while, and then last week he started in again. Jule's is closed on Wednesday nights—that's when Evan used to make his arrangements. Then he'd follow up on them on Thursday for the weekend. I told him I couldn't do that stuff anymore. Then Jason took over. He kept calling Jule's but Evan wouldn't talk to him. When he finally did, Evan said he got the message and wouldn't bother me again. Then what did he say, Jason?" Dennis asked. Jason just looked at him. "*Then* what did he say, Jason?" Dennis repeated.

"He said, 'Take care of Dennis. He's got a good heart. He just needs some guidance. Maybe you can give that to him,'" Jason said quietly.

Nina was moved by their relationship—there was nothing dirty or sexual about it.

Dennis was trembling now. "When Evan was murdered, I was afraid to say anything," he said. "There'd be questions, a lot of them. I'm not proud of what I did, but I know I'm not the only one in this city who got their head turned by some easy money. Jason helped me get my act together. It's part of the past now, but if I came out with all this, I'm pretty sure Mrs. Meyer would have given me the heave. She might have fired Jason, too. Then after Mr. Krueger was a big suspect and Rose was killed, I got real scared. I told Jason we should talk to somebody, but we didn't know who."

"We didn't think we knew anything that would

help Horst," Jason said. "I was protecting myself and Dennis by keeping a lid on our connection to Greer. I guess we're sort of in your hands now, Nina. What are you going to do?"

"Leave," Nina said, rising. She went to Dennis and put her arms around him. "I'm sorry. No one should have to go through what you did. But you're right—you're not the first and you won't be the last. We just need more people in the world like Jason, don't we?"

Dennis was moved to tears. "Yeah. Yeah, we do. Thanks, Ms. McFall. I owe you. I'm real sorry about Mr. Krueger. I think he's innocent, too."

"Greer had to have made a lot of enemies," Jason said. "And a lot of enemies make for a lot of motives."

Nina thought about the brooch. On impulse, she pulled it out of her purse and showed it to the men.

"Getting pretty attached to that thing, aren't you, doll?" Jason said, some of his old humor showing through.

"Maybe more than I'd like to," Nina replied. She saw their puzzled expressions.

"Listen, I don't want to go into all this now, Dennis, but could you give me the address of the secondhand shop where you bought this?"

"Sure," Dennis answered. He wrote the information down, handed the paper to Nina, then asked what Nina thought was a curious question. "How's your friend doing? Is he going to be on the show?"

"What friend?" Nina said.

"The young guy. What was his name? Jay? He came down to props the other day. He seemed real nice. We talked for a long time."

"I talked to him, too," Jason said. "I got the impression he's more interested in what goes on behind the scenes than being on camera."

"What made you think of him?" Nina asked.

"Oh," Dennis replied, "the secondhand shop. We started talking about where I found props and things. I told him what a find I'd just made with the brooch. He wanted to know where the place was, too. Have you heard from him?"

"No," Nina replied. Suddenly she thought she understood why.

Nina quickly said her good-byes, assuring Dennis and Jason that they had nothing to worry about. She believed in their innocence, would keep their story to herself, and in an indirect way they might have told her something that would help Horst.

On her way back uptown, she drove by the secondhand shop. The area was very deserted. Nina pulled up to the curb. Leaving the motor running and locking the doors, she sidled over to the passenger's side of the car and looked at the shop. It was dark, of course. But there was a hand-lettered sign taped to the window of the door: Closed for Vacation.

For some reason, Nina didn't believe that was true. She quickly slid back to the driver's seat, gunned the engine, and headed for home. She had just remembered one of the phone numbers on the phone company's list.

The area code was Boston—the home of the Borden family.

Chapter Sixteen

Nina parked her car in the parking garage under Primrose Towers. When she made her way to the below-ground elevator, she saw Willy and one of the security guards watching her approach. They looked worried.

"Hi, Ms. McFall," Willy said.

"Hi, Willy, Raymond. Something wrong?"

"Looks like a false alarm. One of the other tenants who came home earlier said they saw somebody hanging around the elevator here. They said it was a man, kind of tall, wearing a dark coat and gloves. Sounded odd 'cause it's too warm to be wearing gloves. But there's no sign of him now."

"Glad to see you're on the job," Nina said, hiding her concern. She used her key to get into the elevator. A prowler. Coincidence, or did it make more sense than Nina liked to admit? All the puzzle pieces were there now, and they did form a picture, but Nina just hated the sight of it.

Upon entering her apartment, she was very careful, but seeing Chessy pad over to greet her with his customary yowls and purrs allayed her fears. She knew that Angela had been right—someone *had* been in the town house the night Evan was killed. And Nina also knew, or was at least 98 percent sure, what that person had been looking for.

She laid down her purse and took out the velvet package, then folded back the corners of the dark cloth, unveiling the brooch that was part of the Black Rose. She studied its brilliance, remembering Bernie's words about the ruby's supposed ability to forecast the imminent future of the owner. The red stones were clear and fiery. Nina was not overly superstitious, but she sighed in relief, nevertheless— after all, for all intents and purposes, she was the brooch's present "owner."

She set down the brooch and went to the phone list. Yes, there it was. Two days before Evan's death he'd made a call to Boston. And right after it, another long-distance call—she didn't recognize the area code.

Nina realized this was all conjecture. She could be forcing together pieces of the puzzle that didn't really fit. She could be accusing an innocent man. She could also be wasting time.

Nina went to the phone and, momentarily ignoring the indicator light that said she had messages on her answering machine, dialed the Boston number. The phone rang four times before someone picked up.

"Borden residence," a male voice said in richly formal yet impassive tones. Nina guessed it was a member of the household staff.

"I'm sorry," Nina said. "I seem to have dialed the wrong number." She hung up without waiting for a reply. That certainly supported *one* of her theories. Evan evidently had been on the trail of the brooch somehow even before Angela had worn it to the club. And it was after Angela had taken off her cape to reveal the brooch that strange things had begun to happen. Nina might have picked up more at the time if she hadn't been so thrown by the sight of the blood-red jewels.

Nina looked at the second number, then resolutely dialed. Again the phone rang several times before it was answered.

"Bethel Park State Hospital," a woman's crisp voice said.

Nina hesitated. She certainly hadn't expected to reach a hospital.

"Hello?" the woman asked.

"Yes," Nina said, frantically searching for something to say. "I'm still here." She needed time to think, so she started scratching the mouthpiece with her fingernail. "Hello?" Nina said, turning her face away. "Hello? We seem to have a terrible connection. I'll try again." She scratched a few more times for good measure, then hung up.

Bethel Park State Hospital. Nina knew of another state institution—Hudson River State Hospital near Hyde Park, 90 miles upstate. It was a facility for the insane, hopeless cases, most of whom would never be released into society again.

And then, she realized, that fit into the picture, too.

What had Jay said in Nina's dressing room? Something about people who were too "far gone" to be helped. What else? That they either rotted in a place like that or put on a convincing act to get out. Who was he referring to? A family member? Himself?

Nina began to pace, mentally going over Jay's comments and actions. His mood had altered drastically after Angela had unveiled the brooch. He knew she'd wear it home, but had he expected Evan? Had Evan expected *him*? Dino said Jay hadn't been at Jule's when he went there to question people after Evan was killed. Jay had pointed the finger at Rose—

then she died. Convenient, except Jay hadn't realized at that point that Horst was a suspect—he'd told Nina that. The mysterious prowler at Angela's after Evan was killed—Jay, looking for the brooch, thinking Angela had it. Then Nina told Jay it was a prop, so Jay showed up at the studio, trying to find the brooch in either costumes or props. But it wasn't there. Jay didn't realize Nina had it. Or maybe he did, and rifled the office files looking for Nina's home address. Jay said he was from Boston. Olivia needed a birth record in order for him to be able to appear on the show. If his real last name was Borden, it might have been very sticky. Jay said he came to New York five years ago. It all made sense! "Bethel Park" or "Borden" could have been on that missing page in Evan's address book. Jay could have removed it the same night Evan was killed, just in case.

Nina hurried to the phone and dialed the hospital's number again. The same woman answered the phone. This time Nina knew what she was going to ask.

"I'm calling to check on a patient," she said.

"I'm sorry," the woman replied. "Anyone who could help you with that information is gone for the day. But if you'll give me the patient's name, I could give you his or her doctor's number and you could speak with them directly tomorrow morning."

Nina didn't want to wait that long, but she *did* want confirmation of her suspicions. "Actually, I believe he's an ex-patient, but I would like to speak with the physician, if possible, in any event. The name is Benedict—Jay Benedict."

"Just one moment, please."

The woman pushed the hold button, leaving Nina in limbo. She had to get this information to Dino, if indeed she got any at all. Maybe there was no file. Maybe Jay was never there. Maybe the Borden family had given his physician strict orders to say nothing.

And why would he have been in an institution in the first place?

"Hello?"

"Yes," Nina said, "I'm still here."

"I'm sorry that took so long, but I'm new here and I don't know the filing system or procedures very well. The patient's name was J. Benedict?"

"Yes."

"J. Benedict has a current file. She isn't an ex-patient."

Nina was too shocked to speak for a minute. Finally, "*She?*" she repeated.

"Yes—Julia Benedict. I'm sorry, it's the only Benedict, initial 'J' we have. Isn't that who you were calling about? I told you I was new here. Maybe . . ."

"No, that's quite all right," Nina said quickly. "You've been very helpful. Thank you." She hung up and stared into space. Julia Borden. Julia Benedict. Jay Benedict. Jay Borden. Bernie had said something about Julia Borden and her dock-worker lover having a child. Could Jay be Julia Borden's son? Julia—the black sheep. Somehow driven mad? By what? The Black Rose?

Nina decided she had to call Dino. She hurriedly dialed the number of the station house, only to learn that Lieutenant Rossi was not available. He was out of town working on a case. Charley Harper wasn't there, either. Damn! Why had Dino left town without telling her? Where had he gone?

She remembered the messages waiting to be heard and pushed the rewind button—there seemed to be a lot of calls. The first three were all blank. She listened with growing frustration and fear.

Then her doorbell rang. Nina froze. "Who is it?" she called.

"Security, Ms. McFall. It's an emergency."

Nina ran quickly to the door. She undid the lock

and as she reached for the knob, intending to open the door only a crack, it was suddenly flung open, knocking her totally off balance.

There in the doorway, wearing a dark coat and gloves, stood Jay.

Nina tried to scream, but he was too fast. He quickly grabbed her and covered her mouth with his hand, slamming the door behind him with one foot.

"Don't scream. I won't hurt you," he whispered. "Please, Nina. I need your help! There's not much time."

Nina stopped struggling. This was the last thing she expected to hear. She stared up at him with wide eyes. His cheek was badly bruised, as if he'd been in a fight.

"You won't scream?" he said softly. The haunted look was there in his eyes. But it wasn't madness—it was anguish. Nina nodded. Slowly, Jay's strong grip relaxed. She backed away from him, but he made no move to follow. Chessy appeared, his tail three times its normal size. He looked at Jay and hissed, springing between Nina and her attacker. "I won't hurt you, please believe that," Jay assured her again.

"How—how did you get up here?" Nina managed, catching her breath.

"I had to exert some force on your doorman. Right now he looks like he's sleeping. But he won't be out for long. I saw you drive in. I thought you'd never get home! We have to hurry!"

"I don't understand," Nina said weakly.

"He hasn't called you?" Jay asked, confused.

"Who?"

"I need the brooch, Nina, please. Once he gets it, it will be over. I don't care what happens then!"

The phone rang. Nina had left the answering machine off while listening to the messages, so it wouldn't pick up the call.

"Answer it," Jay said. "I know who it is. I know

what he wants. I've tried to help, but it all went wrong. I won't stand by and see anybody else hurt. I won't! *Answer it!*"

Nina jumped at the tone of his voice. She was totally confused. Nothing made sense to her anymore. With a trembling hand, she picked up the receiver.

"Ms. McFall?" said a deep, familiar voice.

"Yes."

"I know you have the brooch. I want it. I'll exchange it."

"For what?" Nina gasped.

"For Ms. Dolan. She's safe for the moment. But . . . uncomfortable. Don't bring the police. Don't bring anything but the brooch. We'll be waiting for you at Jule's. One hour. No longer."

The line went dead.

Chapter Seventeen

Nina, stunned, hung up the phone.

Jule's . . .

She turned to face Jay. She wasn't sure how he fit into this anymore, but Angela had been kidnapped, Jay knew about it, and he wanted to help. She'd been wrong about Jay—he hadn't killed Evan. He hadn't killed Rose, either. But now she knew who had.

"He's snapped," Jay said. "He's uncontrollable. I've never been afraid of him, not like this." He touched the bruise on his cheek.

"I need to know more," Nina said, "before we go one step further. I already know about the Black Rose. And I know about Julia Borden, or Julia Bene-dict. I know she's in Bethel Park State Hospital. Are you her son?"

Jay gazed at her. After a long moment, he said "Yes," so softly that Nina almost didn't hear him.

"And Dominic?" Nina asked. "That *was* him on the phone, wasn't it?"

Jay nodded. "Dom's my father. I can't imagine how you know about the Black Rose, but since you do, you probably know that my mother ran off with Dom. That was twenty-six years ago. My father used the jewels to build a new life behind my mother's back. He hated her family and everything they stood for. That's why he took the jewels my mother had brought with her. He thought it was some kind of ironic justice. Once he'd made his fortune, he was going to marry my mother and settle in Boston, rubbing her family's nose in his success.

"My grandmother had always hated the legacy those jewels represented, and she was the one who helped my mother run off with Dom and enabled her to take the gems with her, along with her own heirloom wedding gown."

Jay wandered into Nina's living room as he continued.

"I was seven when Dom finally proposed to my mother. I was excited—not many kids get to be best man at their parents' wedding! My mother wanted to wear the Black Rose jewels for the ceremony, a private affair to be held in our lavish home in Pittsburgh. But by that time, the only original piece of the suite left was the stickpin. Up till then, Dom had kept the sale of the other pieces a secret from her. How, I'll never know, except that she loved and trusted him blindly. Dom had no choice but to tell her what he'd done.

"She went mad, right there in her mother's wedding gown in their bedroom. I saw it. I saw how she went at him—the tears, the screams. I watched as she ripped the gown from her body and stood naked in front of him, beating his chest and face with her fists. And poor Dom went a little crazy that day, too. He swore he'd recover the jewels for her, no matter how long it took, thinking that would bring his beloved Julia back to him.

"My mother never recovered. There was no wedding. She was examined by every doctor Dom could

194

find. But she retreated further and further into her own world, the world she'd known before she met my father, a time of grace in the Borden mansion on Commonwealth Avenue in Boston. It was a Victorian wonderland, the place where Julia remembered being pampered, sitting by the fire, and listening to old seventy-eight records on an antique gramophone."

"Jule's," whispered Nina.

Jay nodded. "Dom didn't know what to do with me, so I was eventually sent back to the family. No one would acknowledge me, except for my mother's sister. By then my mother had been committed to Bethel Park State Hospital in Pennsylvania. My aunt told me the whole story when I grew older. I felt sorry for my father and wanted to be with him. So when I turned twenty-one I came to New York. But he didn't want to acknowledge me either at first—until he got into a jam. He'd been recovering the jewels, as he'd promised my mother. He had everything now except the brooch and the ring. He was convinced that if he could return the jewels to her, she'd come back to him, whole and loving once again.

"He tracked down the ring and tried to make a deal to buy it, but the owner wouldn't give it up. Then the owner died, and my father got the ring. I learned that he was capable of things I hadn't dreamed possible. He has an incredible power of rationalization when it comes to doing away with people who stand in his way; it's like a war, he said, and he has to win. There are always innocent casualties in war."

Nina remembered Dominic saying something of that sort to her and Dino when he'd been drunk. "He really believes he can bring her back, doesn't he?" she whispered. "Everything upstairs at Jule's is just waiting for her, isn't it?"

"Yes," Jay said. "After the ring incident, I knew I could never leave his side again. I was trapped by my own guilt and love. I figured I could help my father, make him change. But when he bought that house and started to turn it into what you know as Jule's, I realized I'd never be able to do it. It's a shrine to my mother—the life she lived, the life she secretly wanted, the life my father felt he could never be a part of. But he still thought that when he owned the last piece of the suite of jewels he'd soon have his bride, his Jule, back again. They'd live upstairs and live out a Victorian fantasy together. Nothing could stop him now. Nothing."

"But Evan tried?" Nina asked.

"I never liked Evan, never trusted him. My father would leave New York occasionally and go to see my mother in Bethel Park. Evan became suspicious and very, very curious. He never found out who I really was. Part of my deal to stay close to my father was to keep our relationship a secret.

"Evan was relentless. He was always looking for a bargaining edge. Since Dom's living quarters at the club were strictly off limits, Evan surmised it was because he had something to hide. And he did. That's where my father kept the Black Rose jewels. He'd take the pieces out and look at them, and play this old song about a rose living forever. He believed it could. He also actually believed in the healing power of rubies, the myth that the owner was invincible and was given the strength and courage to carry out his obsessive love.

"Apparently Evan found out too much. As far as I can tell, he discovered where my father went on those trips. He made the connection with the Borden family, who donated huge sums of money to Bethel Park, and he finally uncovered the story of Julia and the Black Rose."

"What happened that night?" Nina asked breathlessly.

"Dom had gone to see my mother—tomorrow is

their 'anniversary.' He was going to stay for the whole week, but my mother had a terrible setback. She was normally calm, almost childlike around him, just confused about who he is. But that Thursday it all came back to her. It was almost a re-creation of the terrible scene on their wedding day. My mother's physician told Dom not to come anywhere near her until she could calm down. Dom came home and got drunk—you must have noticed it."

"Yes. It was the first time I saw him. He was at the end of the bar and you went over to him. You seemed to be quarreling."

"We were. He got that way every once in a while when the rage and self-pity took over. Then when Ms. Dolan took off her fur, he saw the brooch—and so did I. Evan saw our reaction and made a dangerous connection. He was thrown, not expecting that or Dom's return, for that matter."

"Jay, I want to hear the rest of this, but first, what about Angela? Do you think Dominic would really harm her?" Nina asked anxiously.

"Yes," Jay said without hesitation. "He told me he couldn't waste any more time. He had to have the brooch tonight. I've been trying to get it for him ever since the night Evan died. I broke into Ms. Dolan's apartment, used you to get into the studio and broke in there, too, trying to find the damn thing. Afterward, I remembered Dennis telling me that it was a prop for *you*. I realized then that you must have it. I didn't want anything to happen to you.

"Dom trusted me. I knew if I could keep things that way, no one else would get hurt. He likes you, Ms. McFall, but right now you're just an obstacle—so is Ms. Dolan. He's using both of you. He told me his plans to kidnap Angela, then call you. I tried to stop him, but he felt I was betraying him, that I had been all along. So he punched me. I fell down the stairs and he just left me there. I could have been dead, for

197

all he knew. He doesn't care. The only person he loves is my mother, and his quest for that brooch is out of control. It's destroying his mind. He can't see anything rationally at all."

"Then what guarantee is there that he'll let Angela go unharmed when he *does* get the brooch?" Jay was silent. "Jay?"

"I can't answer that. But in spite of all he's done, I don't want to see him hurt. I know that once he gets the brooch, he'll take the whole suite of jewels to the hospital and present them to my mother."

"And if she doesn't respond?"

"Then my father's mind will finally snap. But he'll still have to pay for what he's done, and so will I."

"Do you believe seeing the jewels will bring your mother back to reality?" Nina asked.

Jay hesitated. "I did, once. But I don't anymore. It wasn't the loss of the Black Rose that destroyed my mother, it was Dom's betrayal. And there's no way any of us can change that fact."

"Isn't there any way to get through to him?" Nina asked.

"I tried tonight, and failed. The only person who might be able to do that would be my mother. And that's impossible."

Suddenly Nina had an idea—a frightening idea, possibly a dangerous one. "Jay," she said tensely, "what color is your mother's hair?"

Jay stared at her. "Dark, almost black, like mine, but what . . . ?"

"And her eyes," Nina said, cutting him off. "what about her eyes?"

"Yes—they're green."

"Like mine?" Nina asked.

Jay nodded, then frowned, obviously wary. "What are you thinking?"

"I'm thinking that Angela needs help. That *you* need help. And in a strange way, so does your father.

This may be the most harebrained piece of cloak-and-dagger work I've ever done, but right now it's the only game in town. Now listen—this is what I'm going to need *you* to do."

On its black velvet bed, the fire of the brooch flickered, then dimmed, turning the color of dried blood.

Chapter Eighteen

Half an hour later, Jay and Nina were heading for Jule's. Nina let Jay drive while she thought through her plan more thoroughly. Jay was still against her becoming even more deeply involved, but Nina was adamant, saying that the brooch didn't go unless she went with it. He could have taken it from her by force, but he acquiesced. She felt sure then that she could trust him . . . but just how far, she didn't know.

There was no way to get in touch with Dino, no time to explain the whole mystery to anybody. If worse came to worst, Jay promised to get Angela and Nina out safely while Dom left with the suite of jewels. The police could be waiting for him at Bethel Park State Hospital—Dominic wouldn't go anywhere else.

Poor Angela! Her desire for passion, glamour, and Romance had spun a deadly web around them all. Nina remembered the last time she'd seen her, frantic about Horst but hiding it under that outburst about her wig and the Gothic story line. It had been Angela's tirade that had given Nina her bizarre idea.

Driving was slow. The sudden warm weather had produced a thick miasma of fog. How appropriate, Nina thought. Art was going to imitate life tonight. The crucial difference was, the script Nina was basing her scenario on had a happy ending already written. Tonight she'd be ad-libbing as she went along, and how it all would end was anybody's guess.

Nina fiddled with the clasp of the black cape she wore, which completely covered the outfit she had on underneath. She slipped a hand under the cloak and felt for the brooch pinned over her breast. It seemed strangely warm, as if it had fixed itself to her thudding heart, feeding on her blood.

As they drove, she managed to get the rest of the story from Jay. Evan had been digging into Dominic's affairs and history. It wasn't too hard for a man as clever and driven as Evan to come up with the truth. But Dominic had no idea he'd been snooping.

"Evan came to tell Dominic he was going to take his break, go out for some air," Jay said as he drove. "Dom was in kind of a reverie that night, listening to that old song he always played."

"'Ah! May the Red Rose Live Alway'?" Nina asked.

Jay glanced at her. "How did you know?" he asked.

"It obviously made an impression on Evan. He sent Angela roses and included the first few lines of the song on the card that came with them."

"I'm not surprised," Jay remarked. "Dom played it constantly, even piping it over the sound system after everyone had gone home. Then he'd wander through the club alone, listening to it and replacing the red roses on the tables. I've found myself humming it sometimes.

"Anyway, it seems that Rose and Evan had a helluva fight in Evan's office—Dom could hear them through the walls. Rose had seen Angela slip Evan

201

something she thought was a key, and she was sure he was going to her place. He denied it, and called Buck in to remove Rose.

"I had wanted to talk to Dom ever since we'd all seen the brooch, but he refused to see me. Suddenly, Dom was gone. I went into Evan's office, but he wasn't there, either. What I did find were some copies of florists' receipts scattered on the desk. Several of them had Angela's name and address on them. I was pretty sure that's where he'd gone. I threw the receipts away.

"A while later, I checked Dom's living quarters again. I found him staring into the fire. He told me that Evan knew everything and had betrayed him. After living with his own guilt, betrayal was something Dom couldn't stand. Evan had gone to Angela's to get the brooch and somehow use it against Dom. Dom followed him and killed him with a technique he'd picked up when he was in the Korean War. He said Evan knew he was going to die—he'd seen the same look on men's faces during the war. Evan went over to the roses he'd sent Angela and almost embraced them. Dom wanted Evan's death to be instant, merciful, but the actual killing took something out of him. He couldn't wait for Angela to come home with the brooch. That's when he came back to the club. I immediately went to Evan's apartment to see if there was any evidence that could link Dom to his death. I found a notation in his address book: J.B. Beth P.S.H., and a phone number. I ripped the page out."

Jay grew silent for a moment, then said, "I covered for Dom with the police, saying I'd been with him during the time Evan was murdered."

"What about Rose?" Nina asked.

"Rose wasn't supposed to die. Dom went to her place, intending to pay her an incredible sum of money to leave town. He told her she needed a new start, away from all the ugliness that had happened

202

here. He had a plane ticket and had arranged a new identity for her so she'd never be found. But Rose's feelings for Evan were deeper than Dom realized. She was on a binge of pills and alcohol, but she hadn't meant to do herself any harm. She thanked Dom but said she was going to stick around and find out who had killed Evan if it was the last thing she ever did.

"It was. In her condition, she was no match for Dom. Her death was supposed to look like suicide. Another obstacle removed from Dom's path."

"And Buck?"

"Nobody knows where he is. He and Evan were close. Dom and I have been holding our breath, hoping they weren't so close that Buck knew something. Or maybe he did and couldn't prove it."

Now they were only a block away from Jule's. It was well after midnight on Wednesday and the club was closed. The area was deserted except for the fog that swirled in the streets like restless ghosts.

Jay brought the car to a stop and turned to look at Nina. "Are you sure you want to go through with this?"

"It's too late to back out now," she said grimly. "My first concern is Angela."

"I understand that. But I can't guarantee how Dom will react when he sees you. I can't prep you any more than I have because I know so little about what went on between them in private. I only remember what I told you she used to call him."

"Let's hope that and my talent for improvisation will be all I need," Nina said, sounding a lot more confident than she felt.

"You're a very brave woman."

"I feel like anything *but* right now, Jay. But I have to do this."

Jay peered into the fog that enveloped the car. Nina had the uncomfortable feeling the fog was peering back. "Let's go," he said.

He jumped out, ran to the passenger door and helped Nina onto the street, then led her around to the back entrance of Jule's. He nervously fumbled with a set of keys, quietly opened the door, and entered, Nina at his side. A dim fluorescent light revealed that they were in a storeroom which looked as if it might have been part of the servants' quarters at one time.

"Do you have any idea where he might have put Angela?" Nina whispered.

Jay shook his head. "Dom will probably be waiting downstairs for you in the foyer. I'll watch him while you go up the back stairway to see if Angela's on the third floor. Do you remember the layout I explained to you?"

"I think so."

"All right. Give me thirty seconds, then go." Jay squeezed Nina's hand. "Good luck, Nina. And thanks." He moved off into the shadows. Nina heard his soft tread on the stairs that led to the second-floor kitchen and dining room, then a creak and a gentle *whoosh* that told her he had just gone through the swinging doors.

Nina felt encumbered by her costume, but she didn't want to remove her black cape—it would help her blend into the shadows. She counted to thirty, then found the back stairway and began to climb.

It was cramped and narrow like many back stairs in old houses—not a good place to get caught. She kept moving up, testing each step to make sure it didn't squeak, hoping that Dominic was indeed waiting in the downstairs foyer.

Nina reached a landing and entered a small hallway. She heard a piano and a woman's voice singing, and assumed it was the song about the rose. The brooch seemed suddenly to weigh very heavily on her breast.

As Jay had said, the hallway led to a partially open

door, to what Nina remembered as the game room. When she eased the door open all the way, she saw candles burning everywhere. It seemed that Dom had set the stage for the homecoming of the brooch—and in essence, Julia's homecoming as well.

And that was exactly what Nina planned to provide.

She walked into the game room and suddenly saw herself reflected in a huge, gilded mirror. It was the reflection of a stranger.

Nina saw a woman with dark hair, wearing a flowing cape. She flung open the cape and the candlelight bathed the wedding dress she wore in golden luminescence. The jeweled brooch also caught the dancing flames which stoked its eternal red fire. It burned like a demon's eye, throwing faceted sparks around the room. Nina was transfixed—she didn't recognize herself at all. She hoped when the time finally came, Dominic wouldn't either.

She flowed across the room, parted the red drapes, and checked the foyer. It was empty. The velvet ropes were gone from the third-floor stairway. Moving out from her concealment, she tiptoed to the balustrade and gripped the cool marble like an anchor. Taking a deep breath and gathering up the train of her dress in one hand, she began to ascend the stairs.

Nina was soon outside the door to Dominic's living quarters. She listened, tried the door, and found it unlocked. The sitting room was empty, but the fire burned merrily and there were more flickering candles rapidly diminishing in the heat, their waxy trails spilling down the candelabras.

The gown swishing across the floor behind her, Nina crossed the room and found another door. She gently pushed it inward, to find a huge, lavish bedroom all done in red and black. A canopy bed dominated the scene. Nina noticed that the covers had been turned down, revealing black silk sheets.

Red velvet drapes were drawn across the windows on the far side of the room. More candles burned everywhere, and bouquets of red roses perfumed the air with their cloying scent.

There was a marble fireplace here as well, also banked with a fire. An imposing Victorian sofa stood in front of it, its back to Nina. And lying on the hearth rug, as if casually dropped, was one high-heeled shoe.

Nina raced over and found Angela. At first glance she merely looked asleep, her head turned away, her loose hair covering her face. But on closer inspection Nina saw that her hands and ankles had been tied with red and black silk scarves. She looked like a magician's assistant, ready to be levitated.

Nina bent down and patted her cheeks, whispering her name. When Angela didn't respond, Nina unceremoniously emptied a nearby vase of roses and splashed the water on Angela's face. Angela's eyes flew open, and when they focused on Nina, they grew huge. She opened her mouth to scream, but Nina quickly clamped a hand over her mouth.

"It's me, Angela—Nina!" she hissed. Angela's eyes grew even wider. "Don't ask any questions. I'm here to get you out." Nina hurriedly began working at Angela's bonds.

"Chloroform," Angela muttered faintly. "I can still smell it. I never knew . . ."

"Sssh!" Nina insisted. She freed Angela, who began rubbing her wrists and ankles, still staring at her rescuer. Nina didn't know if it was her ordeal or her growing hysteria that made Angela giddy, but she suddenly started laughing wildly.

"Happy Halloween, darling!" Angela gasped.

"Get hold of yourself, Angela, *please*!" Nina begged in a hushed voice. "I know a back way out. I want you to take it and get away from here as fast as you can. I have to find Jay."

"Jay? . . . What are you doing here all got up like that?" Angela demanded as Nina helped her to her feet.

"I don't have time to explain. Come *on!*"

"My shoe! I paid too much money for them to leave one behind." Nina picked up the pump and fairly threw it at Angela, then began to drag her toward the door.

That's when Nina saw the jewels. She stopped in her tracks and stared. There was a carved wooden chest at the foot of the bed. It was open. The interior was lined with black velvet, and on the velvet rested the companion pieces to the brooch—the Black Rose. She was drawn to them, as if the brooch were actually pulling her across the room, eager to be reunited with its long-lost brethren. She vaguely felt Angela grab her wrist and try to pull her in the other direction.

Then Angela saw them, too. Nina glanced at her and realized that Angela finally understood. It was a buccaneer's dream, a treasure of rubies and diamonds, bearing a legacy of heartache and death. Nina felt an almost overwhelming urge to touch them, but she fought it as if preventing her hand from passing through a flame. And flames they were, at least for a few moments. Then, as a veil of cloud dims the sun, their inner fire was quenched. Despite the heat of the room, Nina's heart turned to ice.

She managed to tear herself away, whispering, "Come on, Angela. It's now or never." Again, Nina felt something tugging at her, begging her to remain, but she resisted it and they left the room. The two women stealthily made their way through the sitting room, into the hall, and finally down the stairs. Angela was still a little shaky, so the going was slow. They were about to part the drapes and enter the game room when they heard movement inside.

Nina didn't hesitate. She grabbed Angela's hand and they raced across the foyer, heading for the other

207

archway. Angela balked, wanting to go down the grand staircase, but Nina roughly pushed her through the drapes. Angela lost her balance, tripped over something just inside the room, and screamed. Nina followed and found Angela in a heap, hands over her mouth in horror. Nina saw what she'd fallen over. Though the body was face down, she recognized the long blond hair and the shearling coat. It was Buck. A red circle of blood blossomed on his back.

Nina nimbly stepped over him, forcing down the feeling of nausea that gripped her. Whoever was in the game room must have heard Angela scream. Nina dragged her to her feet. Angela took one step and groaned in pain.

"My ankle! I've wrenched it! Where are we going?"

"Down the back stairs," Nina hissed. "Get moving!"

"I can't walk down stairs now," Angela moaned. "Back ones *or* front ones." She leaned against a massive wing chair.

Suddenly the drapes parted. Angela gasped, but Nina sighed in relief. It was Jay. Nina knew he had seen them, but he was staring now at Buck's body. She went swiftly over to him and touched his arm.

"Jay?" she said. He slowly looked at her, eyes glazed.

"I was just in the game room looking for you," Jay mumbled. "I heard Angela scream. He's got a gun. He's ranting about betrayal. Buck came here looking for proof that he killed Evan. He got it."

"Where is Dominic?" Nina asked.

"I don't know. I found him downstairs in the parlor after I left you. Something's wrong—he's trashed the entire downstairs of the house on some manic rampage. He wouldn't talk to me—acted as if I wasn't there. I yelled at him to get his attention. He picked up a vase of roses and flung it at me. By the time I got my wits about me, he'd disappeared. We've got to get the two of you out of here. Angela's safe—there's no need to go through with this anymore."

"Angela's hurt," Nina said. "I'll need help getting her downstairs."

Jay looked at Nina, eyes brimming. "I can't leave him," he said simply.

"I just need to rest a minute, Nina," Angela called softly. "Then I'll *crawl* out of here if I have to!"

Nina and Jay guided Angela to a darkened corner and let her sit on the couch. She was wearing a beige silk suit that would be easily seen, even in the dark. Nina took off her cape and ordered Angela to wrap herself in it. Jay was solicitous of Angela, but very quiet.

"God, how I wish I had a drink!" Angela said. "Something to numb the pain in my ankle. I could move a lot sooner."

"Stay here," Nina whispered. "I'll get something from the bar. Jay, stay with her." Jay nodded.

Nina listened, then began to move across the room to the bar area. She was standing directly behind a glowing tier of candles when the drapes parted and Dominic entered. She could only imagine that her expression matched the one on his face. There was only one thing to do. If she was going to play the scene, now was the time to speak her lines.

"Hello, Nicky," Nina whispered, using the pet name Jay had told her.

Dominic stared at her for a long time, then took a step backward.

"Don't you know me, Nicky?" she crooned. "It's me, Nicky. It's Jule. I've come back to you."

Chapter Nineteen

Nina stood very still, praying that the illusion would make him forget everything else. Slowly Dominic took one step toward her, then stopped and cocked his head.

"Nicky? Aren't you glad to see me?"

"It's impossible," Dominic said. "You can't be here!" The words seemed to come from someone else. His lips barely moved.

"But I am, Nicky," Nina said, trying to keep the apprehension she felt from coloring her voice. She realized her hands were trembling and remembered an old acting trick. Use a prop. Keep your hands busy, work your tension into the object. She selected a rose from the vase on one of the tables and took a step forward. She had to get Dominic out of the room long enough for Jay to help Angela escape. But would she be able to do it?

"Look what I've brought you, Nicky," she said, delicately fingering the brooch. Dominic's eyes blazed. In them, Nina saw hatred, then fear, and finally something unfathomable.

"There's still time," he murmured.

210

Nina wasn't sure what he meant by that. Trying frantically to think of something to say, she circled around the room, hoping to make him turn his back to the shadowed corner where Jay and Angela crouched in silence.

"Of course there's time. We have nothing but time now, Nicky. We can be married. No one has to hurt anymore." Dominic's eyes were no longer on her face but on the brooch. Nina was to the side of him now and backing toward the archway. He was watching her closely, like a bird of prey. Something was going wrong. What, she didn't know. "Come with me, Nicky— upstairs. Please."

Dominic started toward her. Nina kept backing up, then felt her foot hit something—Buck's body. She tried to sidestep it, but her foot landed on his outstretched hand instead. She felt herself falling, and then she heard Buck groan. He wasn't dead!

The rose flew out of her hand. As she fell, she caught a glimpse of Buck's face slowly turning to look up at her. A thin trickle of blood came from his mouth. Nina screamed as she saw him reach up to her. His right hand grabbed at the air and finally closed around the train of the wedding gown.

The red drapes helped cushion her fall, breaking away from the rod and falling around her, but trapping her in their folds. Nina struggled to free herself, to reach the foyer, run down the stairs, and try to escape. Then she heard gunshots, and Angela screamed again. My God, she thought, this was turning out horribly wrong!

Free at last from the suffocating velvet, Nina scrambled to her feet and lunged. Buck must have had a death grip on her dress, for she felt resistance. Now Dominic appeared in the archway, a small pistol in his hand, and he was aiming the gun at her. With all her strength, Nina pulled, and heard the heart-wrenching sound of lace and silk being ripped apart.

211

With the tattered train of her dress straggling behind her, she fled for the stairs.

A shot echoed and a piece of marble ricocheted off the first step in a cloud of dust. Nina ducked and threw herself back against the railing, hitting her head on the cold marble. Dazed but still conscious, she saw Dominic advancing toward her.

"Father, stop!" Jay cried, appearing in the archway. Dominic froze. Nina fought a wave of dizziness and began to inch her way to her feet. The railing only went up so far and suddenly Nina felt nothing supporting her back. She gripped the railing from behind to keep from tumbling to the floor below.

"Let me alone," Dominic said to Jay without turning.

"No, you let *her* alone," Jay shot back. "My God, haven't you hurt her enough?"

Dominic looked confused for a moment. "She's dead," he murmured. "My Jule. She's dead. The hospital called." Then the maniacal hatred came back.

Nina felt her blood turn to ice. She'd been impersonating a dead woman! Dominic had been torn by some hopeful delusion at first. Now there was blood in his eyes, as clear and menacing as the ruby brooch had looked when first Nina saw it.

"It's over, Father," Jay said softly. "Please, let it stop."

"It's not over," Dominic said, his steely gaze focused on Nina. He had the gun trained on her breast. She was as rigid with fear as the marble that she clung to. But if Dominic knew his wife was dead, why did he still want the brooch? What possible difference could it make now?

"I can still bring her back!" Dominic screamed, as though he'd read Nina's mind. His voice thundered in the rotunda. "The Black Rose can heal! The Black Rose will bring her back to me. Death will not take her from me. Not yet! The ruby has the power of life!"

"It also has the power of death," Jay said, slowly creeping up behind his father. "The Black Rose has already taken too many lives."

"Only the traitors," Dominic said, spitting out the words. "Only those who tried to keep me from my Jule. They don't understand. *You* don't understand!" Dominic suddenly whirled and pointed the gun at Jay. "You brought her here. You tried to trick me! You've betrayed me! Both of you!"

"Only to save Ms. Dolan, Father. You've got to believe that. We were afraid . . ."

"Afraid of what?" Dominic hissed. "Afraid I wouldn't let her go? Do you think that of your father? Do you think I'd hurt an innocent person? Ms. Dolan *is* innocent—I would have let her go. Don't you understand that?" Dominic suddenly looked struck with pain and guilt. His hand trembled, and Jay made a move forward, but Dominic immediately recovered. "Don't come any closer. You're not innocent anymore. You're one of *them*. You're one of the ones who tried to keep me from my Jule!"

"I'm more than that, Dom," Jay said, choking on the words. "I'm your son. I'm Jule's son. I'm more a part of you than she is. We could have helped her some other way. Now it's too late."

"NO!" Dominic roared. "It's *not* too late! I won't let it be!" He whirled around and advanced on a trembling Nina.

"Freeze! Police!"

Nina couldn't believe her ears. It was Dino's voice! He was running up the marble stairs with Charley! Nina saw Dom turn slowly and raise his gun.

"*No!*" Nina screamed as Jay ran to shield his father. Two shots rang out.

Dominic's shot went wild as Jay knocked into the hand holding the gun, but Dino's bullet hit a mark. Jay spun in pain and gripped his shoulder as Dominic's gun fell from his hand and clattered down the steps to Dino's feet. Nina tried to make a run for it, but Dominic tackled her and knocked the wind out of her.

She was facedown, feeling Dominic's weight on top of her. Her fingers brushed something on the floor—the rose she'd taken earlier. Instinct told her to grab it. She did. The flower was still in her hand as Dominic hauled her to her feet and held her in front of him as a shield.

Nina saw Dino and Charley run up the steps, heard them call out a warning to Dominic to let her go. With one desperate effort, she wriggled free long enough to rake the thorns of the rose across Dominic's face, then dropped the rose and fought to free herself. Dominic cried out in pain as rivulets of blood trickled down his forehead and cheeks. One hand leapt to touch his wounds, but the other held fast to Nina's waist. Suddenly he stared at the blood on his hands, then down at the broken rose, its petals crushed by the heel of his shoe in the struggle.

Nina saw her chance.

"Nicky," she said softly, "Nicky, please . . . let me go." As he stared at her, the madness ebbed from his face, replaced by the memory of love. She felt his grip relax, and pushed with all her strength.

Dominic's back was to the low railing. Nina watched what followed in horrible slow motion. Dominic's flailing hand fastened on the brooch as he teetered backward. The bodice of the gown gave way under his desperate fingers, and the brooch tore free, taking a frayed banner of lace and silk with it. Then, with a wail of anguish, Dominic plunged over the balcony railing.

It might have been a trick of the light or the veil of a shadow, but Nina swore the Black Rose brooch turned dark as night just before Dominic carried it with him to his death.

Chapter Twenty

It was almost four in the morning before Nina found herself back in the safety of her apartment and Dino's comforting presence. She was curled in a chair wearing a soft rust-colored velour robe and sipping a brandy, thinking about the night she'd just experienced.

Dominic was dead, as was Buck. Jay had suffered a flesh wound in his shoulder, but was otherwise unharmed. He would, however, be arraigned on a number of charges involving the deaths of Evan Greer and Irene Rosen, as well as that of another victim of his father's obsession five years earlier. Angela was nursing her bruised ankle.

She and Nina both had given preliminary statements at headquarters, and Nina remembered seeing Dino's professional demeanor crumble as she described what she'd gone to the club to do. She also remembered Angela's haggard face when they were finally allowed to go.

"I don't quite understand any of this yet," Angela had said, "but the hell with it—it can wait. Horst is coming home, and I'm going to be there for him. I really don't know how you manage to survive all this dreadful detecting. Personally, I'm too old for it. But *how old* is our little secret, isn't it, darling?" she added warningly.

Nina had to smile. In spite of all she'd been through, the old Angela was still intact.

Dino explained his miraculous appearance when he drove her and Angela to the station. He'd suspected Jay and Dominic from the beginning. It was mostly a hunch, something he grudgingly acknowledged having picked up from Nina. The conversation he'd witnessed between Jay and Dominic the night he'd taken Nina to dinner at Jule's had disturbed him even further. Delving into Dominic's history, he found some very curious facts, especially about his dock-working days at Boston Harbor, where he'd been brought up on assault charges more than once, all of them involving various methods of Oriental self-defense. Eventually, Dino found out many of the same things that had put Evan Greer onto Dominic's activities. The only thing Dino had lacked was a motive, and Nina had been carrying it with her all along.

Everything seemed to fit into place when Dino followed up on a lead to Bethel Park State Hospital, where he had been when Nina called and was told he was out of town. His conversation with Julia Benedict shortly before her death brought everything into focus, including the legendary Black Rose. He had called Nina to warn her, but she hadn't played back all her messages.

The final ironic twist was Dino telling her that Dom wasn't the sole owner of Jule's. He had a silent partner—Julia's mother in Boston, who secretly believed in the power of the ruby to restore her daughter's sanity. The Black Rose suite would now be returned to its rightful owner.

216

Dino finished his call to headquarters, came to Nina's side, and hunkered down on bended knee in front of her, his gray eyes full of concern and love.

"How are you, babe?" he whispered.

"A lot better than when you found me, love," she answered, caressing his stubbled chin.

"I didn't know it was you at first," Dino said. "Having just left the real Julia, your disguise was a hell of a shock. You really looked like her."

"Right now, I'm content to look like *me*, tired and frazzled though I may be." She paused, and their eyes met. "It was a crazy thing to do, Dino, I know. But Angela . . ."

"Sssh. No judgment calls. Let's just forget this one and move on."

Nina looked across the room and her eyes fell on the tattered remains of the wedding gown. God, she'd have some explaining to do when she showed it to Jason! She glanced back at Dino and realized he was gazing at the dress, too. She remembered Robin wondering what Dino would say if he saw her wearing it.

"You looked very beautiful in that thing," he said. "But not half as beautiful as you'd look in one of your own . . . someday."

Nina held her breath, but he didn't pursue the subject. No, there'd be no proposal from Dino right now. They were still discovering too many things about themselves and their relationship. There were still a lot of bumps in the road ahead, and they both knew it. It was better this way—for now.

"I was guilty of not practicing what I preach," Dino said. "I should have told you up front what I suspected about Startoni and Benedict, but . . ."

Nina placed a finger against his lips. "No judgment calls, remember?" Dino nodded. He rose to his feet and drew Nina up next to him, his face close to hers.

217

"Ever thought about chucking it all and running away to some vine-covered cottage where I could just fish all day and talk to the grandchildren long distance and you'd grow flowers and make cute little pies for dinner?" he asked, grinning.

"What?" Nina exclaimed.

"Nothing. Forget it. It's a fantasy. We'd both grow old before our time out of boredom."

"I don't know," Nina said softly, toying with his crisp, dark hair. "I guess we'll just have to wait and see . . . at least until Peter's old enough to have children, anyway."

Dino brushed his lips against hers.

"As for boredom," Nina said, "you talked about the days, but you didn't suggest how we might occupy the nights."

Dino held her at arm's length. "I thought that was obvious."

"It's not," she said coyly as his hands deftly untied the sash that held her robe around her naked body.

"Then let me show you," he whispered huskily. He kissed her lips and ran his thick fingers through her luxuriant red-gold hair, then smiled. "After all," he said, "if we have to wait so long for our fantasy to come true, let's not get rusty for lack of practice."

Nina let out a giddy giggle that Dino smothered with a passionate kiss.

"Just one thing, love," she said just before he carried her off to the bedroom.

"Anything."

"For a while, at least . . . don't buy me any red roses!"

In Book Six of Eileen Fulton's
Take One for Murder . . .

Nina decides to get away from the glitz, glamour—and danger—of her hectic life in Manhattan, and rents a summer house in the quaint little town of Fox Hollow in upstate New York for a long-overdue vacation. She loves the rambling old clapboard farmhouse surrounded by a lush garden, meadows, and woods. It's the perfect place to relax and unwind. In such a peaceful setting, what could possibly go wrong?

As it turns out, plenty.

On Nina's first night alone in the house, she hears someone prowling around outside, but manages to shake off her apprehension—until she learns that a beautiful young girl who once lived in the house was strangled ten years ago, and her killer is still at large. Nina is glad when Robin Tally joins her for some R and R of her own, thinking that the two women will be able to look out for each other. But Robin's in bad emotional shape. She and Rafe have finally broken up for good, and she's not the most cheerful housemate Nina could wish for.

Then Dino pays a surprise visit—he's taken some time off while Peter is at summer camp. Things seem to be looking up at last, as he and Nina become involved in small-town life. But they soon discover that everyone seems to have some connection with the murdered girl, and that among the Fox Hollow folks there are some very suspicious characters indeed. And when Robin is almost choked to death, Nina and Dino resume their sleuthing partnership to find her attacker before he adds another victim to his list.